In this novel, the first draft of which was written in the depression Thirties and rooted deeply in the emotion of that decade, Tillie Olsen has produced a book both timeless and hauntingly timely. The Holbrooks, a family brutalized by poverty, migrate from a coal mining town to a farm to an industrial city in search of a more tolerable life. The sources of human endurance and hope, the maiming power of circumstance, are profoundly revealed through characters transformed into alive human beings who become a lived experience for the reader. Anna Holbrook, the mother of the family, emerges as one of the most believable and enduring women in American literature. Set aside for nearly forty years, and thought lost, portions of the book were unexpectedly found and the reconstruction of this novel necessitated in the author's words, "the work of this older writer in arduous partnership with that long-ago younger one" to reclaim the book.

Nebraska born, TILLIE OLSEN has lived in San Francisco most of her life. Her widely anthologized book *Tell Me a Riddle* (a Delta Book) is regarded as a modern masterpiece. She has taught at Amherst College and Stanford University; has received Ford Foundation and National Endowment for the Arts awards; was Writer-in-Residence at M.I.T.; and was Distinguished Visiting Professor at the University of Massachusetts.

"This novel is a classic."—*San Francisco Examiner*

Other Books by Tillie Olsen

TELL ME A RIDDLE

SILENCES

YONNONDIO
FROM THE THIRTIES

by Tillie Olsen

A Laurel Edition
Published by
Dell Publishing Co., Inc.
1 Dag Hammarskjold Plaza
New York, New York 10017
A portion of Chapter I was published as
"The Iron Throat" in the second issue,
Volume I of *Partisan Review* in Spring, 1934,
and was reprinted by *Aphra* in the second issue,
Volume III, Summer 1972.

ISBN: 0-440-39881-9

Reprinted by arrangement with Delacorte Press/
Seymour Lawrence, New York, New York.
Manufactured in the United States of America
First Laurel Printing—March 1975
Second Laurel Printing—June 1975
Third Laurel Printing—August 1977
Fourth Laurel Printing—June 1979

For Jack

Yonnondio

Lament for the aborigines . . . a song, a poem of
itself—*the word itself a dirge . . .*

Race of the woods, the landscapes free and the falls.
No picture, poem, statement, passing them to the
    future:
Yonnondio! Yonnondio!—unlimn'd they disappear;
To-day gives place, and fades—the cities, farms,
    factories fade;
A muffled sonorous sound, a wailing word is borne
    through the air for a moment,
Then blank and gone and still, and utterly lost.

from Walt Whitman's "Yonnondio"

The time at the opening of this book is the early 1920's;

the place: a Wyoming mining town.

ONE

The whistles always woke Mazie. They pierced into her sleep like some guttural-voiced metal beast, tearing at her; breathing a terror. During the day if the whistle blew, she knew it meant death—somebody's poppa or brother, perhaps her own—in that fearsome place below the ground, the mine.

"God damn that blowhorn," she heard her father mutter. Creak of him getting out of bed. The door closed, with yellow light from the kerosene lamp making a long crack on the floor. Clatter of dishes. Her mother's tired, grimy voice.

"What'll ya have? Coffee and eggs? There aint no bacon."

"Dont bother with anything. Havent time. I gotta stop by Kvaternicks and get the kid. He's starting work today."

"What're they going to give him?"

"Little of everything at first, I guess, trap, throw switches. Maybe timberin."

"Well, he'll be starting one punch ahead of the old man. Chris began as a breaker boy." (Behind both stolid faces the claw of a buried thought—and maybe finish like him, buried under slaty roof that the company hadn't bothered to timber.)

"He's thirteen, aint he?" asked Anna.

"I guess. Nearer to fourteen."

"Marie was tellin me, it would break Chris's heart if he only knew. He wanted the kid to be different, get an edjication."

"Yeah? Them foreigners do have funny ideas."

"Oh, I dunno. Then she says that she wants the girls to become nuns, so they won't have to worry where the next meal's comin from, or have to have kids."

"Well, what other earthly use can a woman have, I'd like to know?"

"She says she doesnt want 'em raisin a lot of brats to get their heads blowed off in the mine. I guess she takes Chris's . . . passing away pretty hard. It's kinda affected her mind. She keeps talkin about the old country, the fields, and what they thought it would be like here—all buried in da bowels of earth, she finishes."

"Say, what does she think she is, a poet?"

"And she talks about the coal. Says it oughta be red, and let people see how they get it with blood."

"Quit your woman's blabbin," said Jim Holbrook, irritated suddenly. "I'm goin now."

Morning sounds. Scrunch of boots. The tinkle of his pail, swinging. Shouted greetings to fellow workers across the street. Her mother turning down the yellow light and creaking into bed. All the sounds of the morning weaving over the memory of the whistle like flowers growing lovely over a hideous corpse. Mazie slept again.

Anna Holbrook lay in the posture of sleep. Thoughts, like worms, crept within her. Of Marie Kvaternick, of Chris's dreams for the boys, of the paralyzing moment when the iron throat of the whistle shrieked forth its announcement of death, and women poured from every house to run for the tipple. Of her

kids—Mazie, Will, Ben, the baby. Mazie for all her six
and a half years was like a woman sometimes. It's living like this does it, she thought; makes 'em old before
their time. Thoughts of the last accident writhed in her
blood—there were whispered rumors that the new fire
boss, the super's nephew, never made the trips to see if
there was gas. Didn't the men care? They never let on.
The whistle. In her a deep man's voice suddenly arose,
moaning over and over, "God, God, God."

The sun sent its grimy light through the window of
the three-room wooden shack, twitching over Mazie's
face, filtering across to where Anna Holbrook bent
over the washtub. Mazie awoke suddenly; the baby was
crying. She stumbled over to the wooden box that held
him, warming the infant to her body. Then she dressed,
changed the baby's diaper with one of the old flour
sacks her mother used for the purpose and went into
the kitchen.

"Ma, what's there to eat?"

"Coffee. It's on the stove. Wake Will and Ben and
dont bother me. I got washin to do."

Later. "Ma?"

"Yes."

"What's an edication?"

"An edjication?" Anna Holbrook arose from amidst
the shifting vapors of the washtub, and with the suds
dripping from her red hands, walked over and stood
impressively over Mazie. "An edjication is what you
kids are going to get. It means your hands stay white
and you read books and work in an office. Now, get
the kids and scat. But dont go too far, or I'll knock
your block off."

Mazie lay under the hot Wyoming sun, between the

outhouse and the garbage dump. There was no other place for Mazie to lie, for the one patch of green in the yard was between these two spots. From the ground arose a nauseating smell. Food had been rotting in the garbage piles for years. Mazie pushed her mind hard against things half known, not known. "I am Mazie Holbrook," she said softly. "I am a-knowen things. I can diaper a baby. I can tell ghost stories. I know words and words. Tipple. Edjication. Bug dust. Supertendent. My poppa can lick any man in this here town. Sometimes the whistle blows and everyone starts a-runnen. Things come a-blowen my hair and it is soft, like the baby laughin." A phrase trembled into her mind, "Bowels of earth." She shuddered. It was mysterious and terrible to her. "Bowels of earth. It means the mine. Bowels is the stummy. Earth is a stummy and mebbe she eats the men that come down. Men and daddy goin' in like the day, and comin out black. Earth black, and pop's face and hands black, and he spits from his mouth black. Night comes and it is black. Coal is black—it makes a fire. The sun is makin a fire on me, but it is not black. Some color I am not knowen it is," she said wistfully, "but I'll have that learnin' someday. Poppa says the ghosts down in the mine start a fire. That's what blowed Sheen McEvoy's face off so it's red. It made him crazy. Night be comen and everything becomes like under the ground. I think I could find coal then. And a lamp like poppa's comes out, but in the sky. Momma looks all day as if she thinks she's goin to be hearin something. The whistle blows. Poppa says it is the ghosts laughin 'cause they have hit a man in the stummy, or on the head. Chris, that happenened too. Chris, who sang those funny songs. He was a furriner. Bowels of earth they put him in. Callin it dead.

Mebbe it's for coal, more coal. That's one thing I'm not a-knowen. Day comes and night comes and the whistle blows and payday comes. Like the flats runnin on the tipple they come—one right a-followen the other. Mebbe I am black inside too. . . . The bowels of earth. . . . The things I know but am not knowen. . . . Sun on me and bowels of earth under . . ."

Andy Kvaternick stumbles through the night. The late September wind fills the night with lost and crying voices and drowns all but the largest stars. Chop, chop, goes the black sea of his mind. How wild and stormy inside, how the shipwrecked thoughts plunge and whirl. Andy lifts his face to the stars and breathes frantic, like an almost drowned man.

But it is useless, Andy. The coal dust lies too far inside; it will lie there forever, like a hand squeezing your heart, choking at your throat. The bowels of earth have claimed you.

Breathe and breathe. How fresh the night. But the air you will know will only be sour with sweat, and this strong wind on your body turn to the clammy hands of sweat tickling under your underwear.

Breathe and breathe, Andy, turn your eyes to the stars. Their beauty, never known before, pricks like tears. You belong to a starless night now, unimaginably black, without light, like death. Perhaps the sweat glistening on the roof rock seen for an instant will seem like stars.

And no more can you stand erect. You lose that heritage of man, too. You are brought now to fit earth's intestines, stoop like a hunchback underneath, crawl like a child, do your man's work lying on your side, stretched and tense as a corpse. The rats shall be your birds, and the rocks plopping in the water your music. And death shall be your wife, who woos you in the brief moments when coal leaps from a bursting side, when a cross-piece falls and barely misses your head, when you barely catch the ladder to bring you up out of the hole you are dynamiting.

Breathe and lift your face to the night, Andy Kvaternick. Trying so vainly in some inarticulate way to purge your bosom of the coal dust. Your father had dreams. You too, like all boys, had dreams—vague dreams, of freedom and light and cheering throngs and happiness. The earth will take those too. You will leave them in, to replace the coal, to bear up the roof instead of the pillar the super ordered you to rob. Earth sucks you in, to spew out the coal, to make a few fat bellies fatter. Earth takes your dreams that a few may languidly lie on couches and trill "How exquisite" to paid dreamers.

Someday the bowels will grow monstrous and swollen with these old tired dreams, swell and break, and strong fists batter the fat bellies, and skeletons of starved children batter them, and perhaps you will be slugged by a thug hired by the fat bellies, Andy Kvaternick, or death will take you to bed at last, or you will strangle with that old crony of miners, the asthma.

But walk in the night now, Andy Kvaternick, lift your face to the night, and desperately, like an almost drowned man, breathe and breathe. "Andy," they are calling to you, in their lusty voices, your fellow workers—it is an old story to

them now. "Have one on us." The stuff burns
down your throat, the thoughts lie shipwrecked
and very still far underneath the black sea of your
mind; you are gay and brave, knowing that you
can never breathe the dust out. You have taken
your man's burden, and you have the miner's
only friend the earth gives, strong drink, Andy
Kvaternick.

For several weeks Jim Holbrook had been in an evil
mood. The whole household walked in terror. He had
nothing but heavy blows for the children, and he struck
Anna too often to remember. Every payday he
clumped home, washed, went to town, and returned
hours later, dead drunk. Once Anna had questioned
him timidly concerning his work; he struck her on the
mouth with a bellow of "Shut your damn trap."

Anna too became bitter and brutal. If one of the
children was in her way, if they did not obey her instantly, she would hit at them in a blind rage, as if it
were some devil she was exorcising. Afterwards, in the
midst of her work, regret would cramp her heart at the
memory of the tear-stained little faces. " 'Twasn't
them I was beatin up on. Somethin just seems to get
into me when I have something to hit."

Friday came again. Jim returned with his pay, part
money, most company script. Little Will, in high spirits
ran to meet him, not noticing his father's sullen face.
Tugging on his pants leg, Willie begged for a ghost
story of the mine. He got a clout on the head that sent
him sprawling. "Keep your damn brats from under my
feet," Jim threatened in a violent rage, while Anna
stared at him, almost paralyzed, "and stop looking at
me like a stuck pig."

The light from the dusk came in, cold, malignant.

Anna sat in the half dark of the window, her head bent over her sewing in the attitude of a woman weeping. Willie huddled against her skirt, whimpering. Outside the wind gibbered and moaned. The room was suddenly chill. Some horror, some sense of evil seemed on everything.

It came to Mazie like dark juices of undefined pain, pouring into her, filling the heart in her breast till it felt big, like the world. Fear came that her heart would push itself out, roll out like a ball. She clutched the baby closer to her, tight, tight, to hold the swollen thing inside. Her dad stood in the washtub, nude, splashing water on his big chunky body. The menacing light was on him, too. Fear for him came to Mazie, yet some alien sweetness mixed with it, watching him there.

"I would be a-cryen," she whispered to herself, "but all the tears is stuck inside me. All the world is a-cryen, and I don't know for why. And the ghosts may get daddy. Now he's goin' away, but he'll come back with somethin sweet but sicklike hangin on his breath, and hit momma and start the baby a-bawlen. If it was all a dream, if I could only just wake up and daddy'd be smilin, and momma laughin, and us playing. All the world a-cryen and I don't know for why. . . . Maybe daddy'll know—daddy knowen everything." The huge question rose in her, impossible to express, too huge to understand. She ached with it. "I'll ask Daddy." To ask him—to force him into some recognition of her existence, her desire, her emotions.

As Jim Holbrook strode down the dirt street, he heard a fine patter-patter and a thin "Pop." He wheeled. It was Mazie. "You little brat," he said, the anger he had felt still smoldering in him. "What're you runnin away from home for? Get back or I'll skin you alive."

She came toward him, half cringing. "Pop, lemme go with you. Pop, I wanna know what . . . what makes people a-cryen. Why don't you tell us ghost stories no more, Pop?" The first words had tumbled out, but now a silence came. "Don't send me home, Pop."

The rough retort Jim Holbrook had meant to make vanished before the undersized figure of Mazie, outlined so clearly against the cold sunset. In some vague way, the questions hurt him. What call's a kid got, he thought, asking questions like that? Though the cramp in his back from working, lying on his side all day, shot through him like hot needles, he stopped and took her hand.

"Don't be worryin your head with such things, Bigeyes—it'll bust. Wait'll you grow up."

"Pop, you said there was ghosts in the mine, black, not white, so's you couldn't see 'em. And they chased a feller, and then when they got him they laughed, but people think it's just the whistle. Pop, they wouldn't chase you, would they?" The fear was out at last.

"Why," chuckled Jim, "I'd like to see 'em try it. I'd just throw them over my shoulder, like this." He lifted her, swung her over his shoulder, set her down. "My right shoulder, or it wouldn't work. And then I'd pin 'em down with the crossbar so they'd have as much chance as a turkey at Thanksgiving. Now, how'd you like to ride to town on poppa's shouldiehorse and buggy, and get served with a sucker?"

Mazie smiled, but her heart was still sad. "Pop, does the boss man honest have a white shiny tub bigger than you and he turns somethin and the water comes out?

Or is it a story? And does he honest have a toilet right inside the house? And silks on the floor?" She held her breath.

"Sure, Bigeyes. And they eat on white tablecloths, a new one, every night."

"How come he aint livin like we do? How come we aint livin like him, Pop?"

Why indeed? For a moment Jim was puzzled. " 'Cause he's a coal operator, that's why."

"Oh"—another wall of things not understood gone up. Something made the difference. A big word. Like what happened to Mis' Tikas when she was cut up. But how could he cut up a mine? His knife would have to be awful big.

"But you could lick him, Pop, couldn't you? Couldn't you lick anybody?"

"Sure." And to prove it he told her an elaborate story of three dogs he fought, each big as a horse, finishing triumphantly, "Now, do you think anybody could lick your daddy?"

"Pop, I can make the bacon when I stand up on the box, and I can wash the baby, honest. Pop, momma says I'm gonna get an edjication, and my hands white. Is that a story, Pop?"

Fillin the kid's head with fool ideas, he thought wrathfully. But she could become a teacher. Aloud— "Sure you are. You'll go to highschool and read books and marry a—" his stomach revolted at the thought of a mine boss—"a doctor. And," he finished, "eat on white tablecloths."

She trotted along. Somehow the question she had meant to have answered could not be clamped into words. They reached the one street. Her dad went into the company store to buy her a sucker. Afterward when he went into the saloon, she slipped out to the culm bank that rose like an enormous black mountain at the edge of the street. One side was on fire and weird; gorgeous colors flamed from it. The colors swirled against the night, reds and blues, oranges and yellows. "Like babies' tongues reachin out to you. Like what happens to the back of your eyes when you close 'em after seein the sun, only that hurts. Like all the world come a-colored," she whispered softly to herself. "Mazie Holbrook is a-watchin you," she whispered, "purty tongues." And gently, gently, the hard swollen lump of tears melted into a swell of wonder and awe.

It was cold and damp. Mazie shivered a little, but the shiver was pleasant. The wind came from the north, flinging fine bits of the coal dust from the culm against her face. They stung. Somehow it reminded her of the rough hand of her father when he caressed her, hurting her, but not knowing it, hurting with a pleasant hurt. "I am a-watching you, purty tongues."

Sheen McEvoy, lurching out of the saloon, saw a fluttering patch of white against the black culm. "Ghosts," he whispered to himself. His throat became dry. A lost ghost, sent out of the mine, and *white*. "God." The wind shivered against him. Against the culm he saw letters of fire dancing a devil's dance. For a paralyzing instant they danced together, writing a mine blowup. They seared Sheen McEvoy's eyes almost with the terrifying pain of the gas explosion that had blown his face off and taken his mind. The culm made a long finger of shadow toward him—the stars pointed, pointed. "No, no," he moaned, "don't make me have to save 'em."

In Sheen McEvoy's mind insanity dwelled, like a caged wind. Sometimes it was a hurricane, whistling crazily, tearing, making whirlpools of thought, driving his body to distorted movements. Sometimes an old forlorn wind, with the tired voice of dead people, barely touching him, creeping along the sensitive surface. Sometimes the wind spoke or laughed in him. Then awful prophecies came to his tongue. To him, the mine was alive—a thousand-armed creature, with ghosts hanging from the crossbeams, ghosts living in the coal swearing revenge when their homes were broken into. Once fire had risen from earth to sky, clutched at his face, borne it away. Looking in the mirror at himself, he thought now some ghost in the coal was wearing it, laughing.

The wind began its whining. He ran unsteadily for the white flutterflutter. Dazed, he saw it was a small child, with unholy eyes, green. A voice spoke in him, "A little child, pure of heart." *That* was it. The mine was hungry for a child, she was reaching her thousand arms for it. "She only takes men 'cause she aint got kids. All women want kids." Thoughts whirled in colors—licking to flame; exultation leaped up in him.

Sheen McEvoy will fill you, ol' lady. His laugh, horrible as the cracked thin laughter of old breastless women watching youth, sent the night unsteady. Mazie looked up. Sheen McEvoy was standing above her, laughing. Her heart congealed. The red mass of jelly that was his face was writhing, like a heart torn suddenly out of the breast, and he laughed and laughed. Mazie wanted to run; her mind fainted on the thought of her father, strong and tall, so far away. She turned to go.

He held her. His body was hot and putrid. Stinking. "You're the mine's baby now," he said, holding her tight. "The mine'll hold ya like that, pretty baby." Screams tore at Mazie's throat, caged there. Sweat poured over her. She closed her eyes. He strode toward the shaft. He kissed her with his shapeless face. In Mazie her heart fainted, and fainted, but her head stayed clear. "Make it a dream, momma, poppa, come here, make it a dream." But no words would come.

Instead another voice, thundering. "What are you doing with that kid, McEvoy?" No words would come. But he—his breath stinking, the jelly opening in the middle. "Stand out of my way. The mine is calling for her baby. Men'll die—unless she gets a baby. Stand back."

The night watchman's mouth came open. "Put her down."

Sheen McEvoy strode on, oblivious. Angels were singing in his head, men were singing—glad praise, saved men. Her body was soft and warm. "Lift my arms and throw her down the shaft and the mine'll forget about men."

"Put her down."

"Give her a sweet baby, and she'll want no more." Angels singing, men, strong-bodied men, marching and singing, saved. Her body, soft, trembled against him. Ecstasy sang. Now the shaft, hungry mouth.

"I am giving you your baby." He lifted his arms. Mazie saw down, but there was no bottom. Her scream sounded now, answered by his laughter: shrill, cracked, horrible.

Darkness came like lightning. His arms loosened. Mazie rolled, barely missing the shaft. Rising, she crawled, toward what she did not know. The tipple rose like a tree, without leaves, above her. Words came, drunken. Fear. "Momma. Poppa." Behind a figure rose, menacing; swung. A miner's pickax. Blindness on two men, fighting. The ax swings, misses. A gun spurts, one, two, three; lovely fire colored like on the culm, colored like the thoughts in McEvoy's head. One instant angels singing, men marching and singing, saved men; the mine yawning, hungry; soft body trembling to him. Blackness now. Black as the day in the mine. Over and over a body lurches, dips into a shaft, thuds thuds against the sides. The clouds, throwing their shadow, give for an instant a smile, inscrutable, to the mouth of the mine.

Into the saloon, like some apparition, came the nightman, bloody of face and clothes, carrying a child. The men looking up from their drink, laughter and oaths cut off, stared astounded. Breathing heavily he walked to the center of the room and asked fiercely, "Whose kid is this?"

The whiskey making giddiness of his veins, Holbrook turned. The oath, so like a laugh, died on his lips. The kid was Mazie. "It's my kid," he answered gruffly. "What the hell are *you* doin with her?"

"You oughta thank your damn guts I am doin something with her. Why didn't you watch her, if she's your kid?"

The whiskey made a lovely golden fog in his head. Not understanding, he lurched to the nightman, taking the kid away. "What you been doin?" he asked sharply. "What did you run away for?" Her eyes opened for an instant. Questioning and impersonal like a wounded animal's, they stared at him. Uncomprehending, meaning to roar some oath, he looked toward the nightman. The tense, accusing face came like a wind, blowing the fog with cold sharp wings. "What happened?" he asked tersely, still shaking Mazie.

"Stop shaking the kid, she can't answer you, she's sick. And who wouldn't be? That bastard McEvoy went on another loony spree. Picked her up somewhere and gets the idea the mine wants a baby, as if it don't get enough grownups. Comes to the shaft laughing and singing about the men he's going to 'deliver.' When I looked for the kid she was crawlin like some blind animal. Scared to death."

"The sonofabitch," roared Holbrook, "I'll kill him. Where is he?"

"Keel him, leench him," one man muttered angrily.

"The mine done the job for you. He fell down the shaft he was aimin to throw her down."

Holbrook felt as if he were drowning. He felt weak, like a child. My baby, this happened too, he thought. He shook her again, but gently. The stirring of her body against him was insufferably sweet anguish.

"Geev her a sweeg dees," one of the Greeks offered roughly. "That waken her up."

"No, Nick, I'm taking her home. Anna'll fix her up. Got a coat, anybody?"

Tenderly he wrapped her in one, letting no one else touch her. Walking home, he still felt as if he were drowning. Once when she opened her eyes and in a dream-voice murmured, "Poppa, you came," tears stung his eyes.

"My baby, this had to happen too." A monstrous thought gripped him. Frightened, he shook her roughly. "What did he do to you, Mazie, Bigeyes, what did he do to you?" He ran for the yellow light that made a neat block on the road.

Anna was still by the window sewing, in the attitude of a woman weeping. But her eyes were tearless—they shone at him like hard bright steel. "You're home early. Get homesick?"

Remorse added to terror and shame. "Anna," he said, so broken, so tender, her heart leapt.

"Jim?"

"The kid. She. Maybe . . ." He could not speak.

"Mazie?" cried Anna, shrill. "What happened? What've you done to her?" She snatched the child, spoke to her, took her to the light. There was a small bruise on her forehead, scratches on her face.

"You beat up on her, you dirty bastard."

"No, listen Anna." He told her the story, tremblingly told his fear. He was like a child. Terrified, he heard Anna's hysterical laughter—then her calm.

"She hasn't been touched. She'd have been all bloody if he had. But God only knows how hurt she is. Put on hot water, you, and bring some whiskey into the bedroom." She carried Mazie onto their cot and tumbled hot whiskey and tea down her throat.

Jim sat and held the lamp. His wavering shadow looked at him from the wall. Feeling Mazie's burning head, her body moist with sweat, he asked, "Shouldn't I get a doctor?"

"Forget where you are? You know there's only the company doc—and a vets better'n him. She'll be all right. Looks like she might've hurt her head fallin, or maybe she's just scared. Poor baby, poor baby, I'll give her more hot whiskey."

The wind, starting up outside, shook against the house, and Mazie in the quiet of the bedroom began crying, tossing, calling out fragments of sentences, incoherent words. Will, waking, saw how his father sat so still and terrible. Still in his sleep, he began to whimper—"dont hit me, Poppa, dont. I didn't mean nothing." Unsteadily Jim stood up. The waters seemed closing over his head again: a grimy face turned up to him, pleading, "a story, Pop," and a hand that had crashed down over it. Almost timidly he rubbed that hand against the soft head. "You're dreaming, Will boy," he whispered. "Sleep agin. Try to sleep."

He turned down the light. The new-made, concealing darkness came welcome to them both. "Listen," he gripped her shoulders, "we're clearin out in spring, you hear? We'll save every cent. We'll go to Dakota. Spring's the time to begin a new life, aint it? I'll farm. That's a good job—I could do it, tried my hand at everything else. Or maybe we'll go to Omaha—get on at the slaughterhouse. No—it'll be farmin, workin with ground, not rock. Ground smells sweet. And it's good for the kids, right, Anna? We'll make it a new life in the spring?"

In her delirium Mazie laughed—terrible laughter, mocking, derisive, not her own. Anna and Jim, hearing it mix with their words, shuddered.

TWO

A new life in the spring. But now fatback and corn-meal to eat. Newspapers stuffed in shoes so that new ones need not be bought, and the washing done with-out soap. Somehow to skimp off of everything that had long ago been skimped on, somehow to find more necessities the body can do easiest without. The old quilt will make coats for Mazie and Ben, Will can wear Mazie's old one. This poverty's arithmetic for Anna, and for Jim—hunger for the gayness whiskey gives the world, battling fear that before spring the mine will en-gulf him.

A new life . . . in the spring. Once Anna tried to tell the children. Illumining her drab words with her glowing face, Anna told them of living among trees, having Daddy work where they all could see him, of a good school—not a Catholic one—and milk from cows. Will, watching her face with burning eyes, said, "That a fairy story, Mom?" but Mazie hardly seemed to listen; crept out of the house, restless, before Anna was through.

The children were changed. Even their "aint there nothing else to eat, mom?" was apathetic. The peace at home, their father so awkwardly gentle, sitting home nights now, frightened them. Always they were expect-ing something else. Mazie sat still the evenings staring into the stove, and when Jim tried to woo her to smiles, she gave him such objective ones, they froze him.

In the coal town too there lived a subtle fear. The new fire boss was the super's nephew, too scared, too lazy, it was said, to go stumbling through the foggy workings alone, testing to find out if gas had collected. In everyone's heart coiled the fear of a blowup. Nights the saloon jetted with fiery laughter, reckless song, hard evil fights. On the women's faces lived the look of listening. And the autumn days, shaken with rain and restless wind, brought always the sound of fear, undefinable, into the air.

One November day the sky was packed so thick with clouds, heavy, gray, Marie Kvaternick said it had the look of an eyelid shut in death. Leaves dashed against the houses, giving a dry nervous undertone to everything, and the maniac wind shrieked and shrieked.

Anna's face that day had the look of a mask, racked listening hidden underneath. It drove the children restless. Even the baby, sensing the tension, whimpered. "Shut baby up," Anna demanded of Mazie. "I dont care how." Mazie gathered him up, with a bread crust for him to suck on, and a diaper, and slipped out. Will came alongside.

Above colors were gathering in the sky. Sunset colors, though it was early afternoon. Mazie remembered the colors in the culm and shuddered. There was a grove away from the town—a long way—but they went there. Will played with his stocking ball, and she lay down in the rustling autumn leaves, one hand over her eyes, shielding them from she did not know what. The baby lay warm in her other arm, there where it ached from carrying him.

High up the wind was whirring, but here there was

only a gentle shadow of it. "All that be here is the end of its skirt," Mazie whispered. And in the darkness of her arm, the tightness that had been around her heart slackened, eased, was no more.

Will came over. Lay down, his head snuggled on her stomach. "Five years. I'm five years old. What be it to be five years?"

"Five years you've lived, Will."

"Five years. I'm wearin your old coat, a girl's coat. For why?"

"For that's all there is. Shush now, let baby sleep. Shush, and hear the wind cryin."

"The wind? What's wind?"

"It's people cryin and talkin."

"People?"

"Yes, people in the sky."

"Sky? What be sky?"

"Shush. That's something I'm not knowin."

"Sky be a winder?"

"Yes, a window."

"You can't see through it, 'cause it's dirty?"

"No, your breath's blowin up on it, everybody's breath—open your eyes and you see it go up and it makes it cloudy."

"Breath? Not rags. Looks like rags stuck in the window, a-flappin."

"Shush Will, not rags. Listen to the leaves. Sounds like people walking quiet, quick—walkin past on tiptoe."

"Fatback tastes in my mouf."

"Eyes closed and you hear better."

"Fatback sour in my mouth. Wish I had a apple."

"Poppa comes home and stays." Something stirred in her breast faint like the leaves about her. Dont think of poppa. Hear the leaves.

"Ask momma for a apple. She says no."

"He never hits no more. Looks at me like he got something good, but never gives it, only looks like."

"Johnny tole me what you eat grows in your belly. I gonna grow fatback."

"And momma . . . bein mad then bein sorry . . . momma always lookin as if she expects to hear something. . . ."

"Grow fatback and be dead. Mazie, what's dead?"

"Momma listenin, always listenin." The tightness had come alive again; it strangled around her heart. She leapt to her feet with a cry, waking the baby. Some terror crept upon her.

"Mazie, whatsa matter?"

She pointed. Above the sky were ears. In all their different shapes they coiled, blurred ears, listening. And looking down, she saw that the wind was pitting the grasses and leaves, making little whirlpools, kitten-shaped ears, listening, listening. The face of her mother, the face of Mis' Connors, the face of Mis' Tikas came like a mist before her eyes—listening, everywhere, everywhere.

"Willie, lets go home, Willie. I'll race you, baby and all. Lets go. Put your hands in your ears and you dont hear nothin, lets go, run."

The wind was icy on her running body; the baby dragged. But everywhere the sky and earth were listening. And the whistle—yes, it was the whistle that was shrieking—not the finger in her ear, not the wind. At the tipple there would be . . . thinking of the tipple, her heart plunged, she wanted to fall, to stuff the leaves into her ears. "Willie, lets run, Willie." He moaned: "Momma be runnin, everyone runnin and screamin, Mazie."

"Lets run away, Will." A thought hung with bulldog

teeth to her mind—"It'll be daddy this time."

"Lets run away," but their feet were flying—flying to the tipple.

The women were there already. Tearless faces, watching. But no one brought up limp and sagging. Instead, frightened men, and the rest sealed in an open grave. A big explosion. It might take days to dig them up. Anna with bloodless lips formed "a new life," but Will and Mazie were pulling at her skirt, her baby was moving in her arms, and Marie Kvaternick hurting her shoulder. "You see, Anna. They be up. These big ones—they save; nothing happen. Only little accidents they die. But if Andy stay—" she pushed out fierce— "if Andy stay, better for Andy. Wots matter, Anna? You see, Jim'll be back, they be up. Only . . . Chris . . ."

And could you not make a cameo of this and pin it onto your aesthetic hearts? So sharp it is, so clear, so classic. The shattered dusk, the mountain of culm, the tipple; clean lines, bare beauty—and carved against them, dwarfed by the vastness of night and the towering tipple, these black figures with bowed heads, waiting, waiting.

Surely it is classical enough for you—the Greek marble of the women, the simple, flowing lines of sorrow, carved so rigid and eternal. Surely it is original enough—these grotesques, this thing with the foot missing, this gargoyle with half the face gone and the arm. In the War to Live, the artist, Coal, sculptured them. It was his Master hand that wrought the intricate mosaic on this face— splintered coal inlaid with patches of skin and threads of rock . . . You will have the cameo?

Call it Rascoe, Wyoming, any of a thousand mine towns in America, the night of a mine blowup. And inside carve the statement the company already is issuing. "Unavoidable catastrophe . . . (O shrink, super's nephew, fire boss that let the gas collect) . . . rushing equipment . . . bending every effort . . . sparing no expense . . . to save—or recover the bodies . . ."

(Dear Company. Your men are imprisoned in a tomb of hunger, of death wages. Your men are strangling for breath—the walls of your company town have clamped out the air of freedom. Please issue a statement; quick, or they start to batter through with the fists of strike, with the pickax of revolution.)

A cameo of this, then. Blood clot of the dying sunset and the hush. No sobs, no word spoken. Sorrow is tongueless. Apprehension tore it out long ago. No sound, only the whimpering of children, blending so beautifully with the far cry of blown birds. And in the smothered light, carved hard, distinct, against the tipple, they all wait. The wind, pitying, flings coal dust into their eyes, so almost they could imagine releasing tears are stinging.

"He'll be back." Brought up quiet and shaken five days later. Gaunt and bearded so that Ben wailed when he saw him. "In March, Anna," he said, "March, if I have to pick the sun outa the sky for a gold piece."

Whispering—"Just give me one third for the scrip. Just one third cash. You know it's worth more than that. I'll buy the stuff for you, so they'll think it's me, and you pay me one third cash."

Pushing the words out from where they stand so humbly in her throat. "I thought maybe around the holidays there might be extra work. Scrubbin or washin. I know you got a cook. I'm not askin much, just fifty cents the day."

Fear. You got no business doin it, Jim, workin under loose roof like that.

But March—a new life . . . And they dont pay for pullin it down and clearin. And I cant do nothin unless I'm gettin paid for it.

"Ma. They growin chicory instead of coffee? Aint we ever gonna have coffee again?"

"Ma, my teef hurts."

"Ma, I can push my finger in Mazie's skin and it goes in, way deep."

"Ma, this all to eat, Ma?"

"In spring, in March, we're goin, baby. Hushabye now. Hushabye. Momma'll sing you to sleep."

March. Raw with blistering winds and snow. I see even the weather's against us. No use, we can't leave. But April. April for sure.

All winter his reckless work under loose roof, because pulling down and clearing meant unpaid labor. All winter the children puffing out with starch. All winter her hands cracking with the extra work.

But the decrepit wagon waits outside, and Jim pounds on an extra rude seat, a rough removable canopy. There is an ancient truck horse bargained for and promised. And sometimes clearing the coal, walking to work in the morning darkness, scrubbing his face, Jim stops suddenly, and thickly out of his throat utters, "April." And Anna's hand goes often over her heart, remembering new-life words of hope spoken against the weave of a delirious child's laughter.

April at last. Delicate with shy greens and little winds blowing. A few of the women come to bid goodbye. And when Anna closes the door for the last time, quick, hard, dropping her hand from the latch, they watch as if it were a ceremony. Wistfulness is in their eyes, no envy. "Goodbye. Goodbye," they chorus. But the Holbrooks do not look back, only Mazie once, but there is nothing left, only a shadow of culm, rearing against the sky. Over it small white clouds forming and dissolving—almost fairy hands, waving goodbye, goodbye.

THREE

Three days they jolted through Wyoming and west Nebraska. The black cuts of the buttes against the sky, the colors in them like striped fire, the great quiet desolation of the mesa they passed, filled Mazie with some strange unhappiness, more like happiness than anything she had ever known. Anna felt like a bride; riding along, she sang and sang. Sometimes Jim whistled or sang with her in a depthless bass voice. And the wagon made gay silvery sounds accompanying them, and the sun laid warm hands on their backs.

The fourth day they came to South Dakota—breaths caught in sharp wonder at the green stretching for miles, at the small streamlets like open silver veins on the ground, and here and there dots of cattle grazing, heads down. The air was pure and soft like a baby's skin. "Breathe," Anna said, "breathe it in, kids." "Listen, Momma, there's birds." Birds, floating round shining bubbles of song on the air, jackrabbits rising suddenly from one end of the road to flee to the other.

And that day there was laughter. Nellie, refusing to trot, stopping stubbornly, haunches apart, head lifted up. In vain Jim beat her. When he clambered down to lead her, she galumphed away at a tremendous (for her) speed. Though Anna, frantic, tried to reach to dragging reins, the children screamed and laughed.

Crazy, the wagon tipped, this side, that side. "Seesaw, Marjorie Daw," Will began. And Nellie, with immense dignity, stopped.

Five minutes later Jim came puffing up. A farmer stopped his plowing to lean over the fence. "Ya oughta get a mule I reckon. They're not so stubborn."

"She *is* a mule. In disguise." Jim climbed up again. But again she wouldn't budge. Leisurely she cropped the grass at her side.

"How about the old grass-on-the-end-of-a-stick gag?" the farmer asked. "That'll start her trottin."

It did. Jim, with one foot on the step, felt the wagon jerk forward and barely swung himself up in time. Nellie didn't wait to go for the food that hung tantalizingly beyond her nose. For two hours she ran, Jim precariously directing her with the reins around corners. Mazie stood up, her hands on the wagon seat, screaming with delight. The wind came over her body with a great rush of freedom; freedom and joy tingled to her hair roots. Anna swayed back and forth, clutching her hat and the baby, laughing too. Ridiculous Nellie with her huge buttocks moving in frenzied rhythm, the wagon bumping along after, and the wheels making their singy laughter. Laughter came from the skies, blowing something that was more than coal dust out of their hearts.

The sky tinged leaden. Enormous shadows began to shift over the face of the prairie, and above the whole sky came gray, with dull silver undersides to the clouds. Cold, the wind whirled from the north. Nellie set her head stubbornly against it, plodding along. Jim stopped to stretch the canopy over them, telling the children to scurry into their coats.

The wind began running a long hand under the dust, stirring it into a dervish dance. A steady moaning came from the grasses. Mazie leaned forward to catch the feel of the wind on her face—something seemed clawing in her to be out running with it. Anna for some reason was laughing.

A cold tongue licked their cheeks—snow. Jim shouted back, "Cover up with them blankets and throw another up here, Mazie. You better go back with the kids, Anna," but she was already there, covering, reassuring them. Mazie crept forward. The sky was invisible now. When she lifted her face, the snow stung like nails. Mistily she could see her father—on his face a look of being intoxicated, his heavy brown hair blowing back, his blue eyes glittering. The snow fell thicker. The wind whirled it like a dancing skirt. Even following the road was difficult. The fences alone helped. And nowhere was there a farmhouse. Mazie did not care—it was enough to stumble on like this forever through a white whirling world. The wagon sank. Nellie pulled bravely but in vain. Jim got out. The back wheels were sunk deep in what had been a spring pool of water, under the snow.

"What's the matter?" Anna's shout came faintly.

"We're stuck," he yelled back—the futility of voices yelling loud but coming out like babies' piping voices obsessed him. With head down Jim pulled against the wind to win to the front of the wagon again. Snow was blowing in from the open front. "It'll be a minute."

Mazie awkwardly fought her way after her dad, watched him lay down in the snow, put his shoulder under the wheel. His body tautened, the wheel jerked. Again he straightened out tense, and the wheel lifted. Jim held the weight of the wagon on him, not knowing what to do next. Slowly he wriggled his body to the right, then crept from under. Mazie could hear his hoarse breathing pulsating with the wind. He was fumbling along the roadside, edging a rock on the ground under the other wheel. "Roll it under when I lift it up again," he commanded. Again, with terrible strength he lifted the wheel. To Mazie, her fingers frozen, rolling the rock seemed to take forever. Trembling, she got it under.

In an hour they found a small town, crouched in a hollow. In a one-story "hotel" run by an obese Swede and his lanky wife, they got shelter. She caressed the children, made a crackling fire, rubbed their hands, put on hot water for footbaths, exchanged recipes with Anna, talked of the marvelous farming country around Zell, where they were going.

Mazie, shivering before the fire, her eyes closed, remembered the feel of the wind and the culm left behind.

The morning was a dim smear of light. Jim, looking at the white country, shook his head. No travelin today. The sun made a wan smile of the afternoon, and all night the melting snow dripped, dripped. Morning came, and the road was clear but muddy. Ben cried at leaving the gaunt lady.

Two days later, the weather shining again, they came to a rise. Looking down, they could see for miles. Far east rolled the hills, the near ones flat brown, washed over with delicate green, the far ones repeating themselves over and over till they faded into blue hazes and dull mists—indistinct blurs of lines against the spring sky.

Below lay the farms, uneven patches of brown and plowed black and transparent green, and far stretched the river, dull yellow in the sun, glinting crystal, where the wind stirred it. Tiny as a toy, a man was plowing a thin thread of black in the brown square of field immediately below them.

Everyone's eyes were shining with wonder and promise. "We'll be living somewhere beyond that," Jim said, with a gesture of joy and freedom illimitable (goodbye, mole's life, goodbye, you're far behind me now); Willie babbled childishly of the man, grown so tiny, and the baby stretched his arms and crowed. One joy lay in their hearts like a warmth—hope. "A new life," Anna said, "in the spring."

With dusk a softness crept over the land. They were down in the lowlands now. Low curves cut into the sky. The earth glowed with reflected color, like light under green water, and Anna and Jim began singing, "Down in the valley, valley so low, hang your head over, feel the wind blow."

Willie slumbered against Mazie's shoulder. Ben drowsily had his head in her lap, staring into the depthless transparent green above. Even the gay tinkle of the wheel came subdued and the clop of Nellie's hoofs incredibly hushed and beautiful. "Roses love nightwinds, violets love dew, angels in heaven, know I love you." Their voices were slow curving rhythms, slow curving sounds. Voices, rising and twining, beauty curving on rainbows of quiet sound, filled their hearts heavy, welled happy tears to Mazie's eyes.

Anna singing, "In the gloaming, oh my darling, when the lights are dim and low," with bright eyes folded and unfolded memories of past years—plans for the years to come. School for the kids, Jim working near her, on the earth, lovely things to keep, brass lamps, bright tablecloths, vines over the doors, and roses twining. A memory, unasked, plunged into her mind—her grandmother bending in such a twilight over lit candles chanting in an unknown tongue, white bread on the table over a shining white tablecloth and red wine—she broke into the song to tell Jim of it . . .

They reached the farm at midnight. Anna had awakened Mazie so she could see. There were flatter fields, low houses, some with towers her father softly pointed out as silos. Sometimes Jim got out and fumbled with a match before a mailbox or signpost. At last there came a low rambling place, with three trees dwarfing it and barn larger than the house looming in the back. Above the stars glistened—and two twin stars hung over the roof. "The place," Jim said.

Mazie, sleepy, lay down immediately on the mattress stretched for her and, with Will and Ben breathing quietly beside her, fell asleep at once. Jim spent another hour getting the barn open, moving the one bed they had taken with in and setting it up while Anna, nursing the baby held in the crook of one arm, unpacked what would be needed for the morning. Then they too slept. And into their sleep wove a dream of beauty curving on rainbows of quiet sound over a land that stretched into mist, in which one figure, tiny as a toy, ploughed a black thread in a square of brown.

FOUR

The farm. Oh Jim's great voice rolling over the land. Oh Anna, moving rigidly from house to barn so that the happiness with which she brims will not jar and spill over. Oh Mazie, hurting herself with beauty. Oh Will, feeling the eggs and radishes gurgle down his throat, tugging the woolly neck of the dog with reckless joy. Oh Ben, feeling smiles around and security.

Well, what of Benson? stoop-shouldered neighbor and his "I tell you, you cant make a go of it. Tenant farmin is the only thing worse than farmin your own. That way you at least got a chance a good year, but tenant farmin, bad or good year, the bank swallows everything up and keeps you owin 'em. You'll see."

But land is here. Days falling freely into large rhythms of weather. Feet sinking into plowed earth, the plow making a bright furrow. Corn coming swiftly up. Tender green stalks with thin outer shoots, like grass. Oh momma come look! Oh daddy come look! Oh Mazie come look! Drama of things growing. You're browning, children, the world is an oven, and you're browning in it. How good the weariness—in the tiredness, the body may dream. How good the table, with the steam arising from the boiled potatoes and vegetables and the full-bellied pitcher of milk.

Around the house, the earth is hoed up for truck. Mazie and Will do the weeding, help feed the chickens, bring the cow from pasture, wring out the clothes. But strangely there is time. Sometimes Mazie pads with bare feet across the waving corn to the road—to watch the carriages and wagons bump by. When there are gay little girls sitting high and proud in the buggies, ribbons in their hair blowing a long streamer in the wind, shame and envy shudder over her, and she draws herself together to make herself nothing, to lose herself in the faded gray dress on her body. Then the sun and wind rippling over her skin, and the gold corn moving against the sky lull her into beauty again with the slenderest arms of rhythm.

Sometimes the neighbors come. Benson, he of the stoop shoulders, as if for all his six feet he were trying to get closer to the earth. Two furrows live on his brow and a curious compassion in his eyes. A compassion that is weariness and despair. He will start to talk of a new way of planting, of the good weather, and then cease suddenly, the compassion gray where the living was before. Missis Ellis, round and laughing, sure of touch, knowing the helplessness of newborn animals, how to bring animals and women out of labor, her voice the timbre of earth. She laughs, but a kernel of worry hides under the laughter. Her father is old Caldwell, pioneer, who had come west from college and wealth and chosen to live and build out of the wilderness.

Jim's big barn was the accustomed place for the midsummer dance in mid-July. Two days before, neighbor women came to prepare the floor, bring food, help with the cooking. Anna sewed over her good dress, bought bright ribbons recklessly for Mazie and herself, washed and starched the children's clothes.

The laughter of summer was on the earth. Trees, rich and voluptuous, flowered by the roadside, brimming fields of corn waved in the sun, roses were in bloom, and the days were bright with the colored balls of song, birds tossed back and forth.

The night of the dance was luminous with moonlight. Winds rushed over the fields, faded to small breezes, subsided into stillness, gathered again. Trees dipped and curtsied, the corn rippling like a girl's skirt. Very low, very misty, very tender, the stars shone, and over all flowered the smell of growing things, of fecund earth, overpowering.

Mazie, with the green ribbon glowing on her head, felt like spring. To her, Anna with her black eyes laughing, her black hair smooth and shiny to purple, was the handsomest woman there. But everyone had a look of beauty about them.

Withered and small, the fiddler seemed too frail for any sturdy music, but at his side the guitar and harmonica player rose strong and capable. The caller stood in the middle. The circle eights formed. Then the music rocked in the air. Some of the dancers were young girls and boys, quick of step, their laughter rising like a froth, quick colors, step on step, bubble on bubble. Most were middle-aged men, women, still young, if not in body. They gave themselves easily to the dance, backs curved, skirts flying round and round. Round and round in the intricate steps, and, at the end of each circle eight, the men gave out a long cry that beat up the blood. Summer was in their hearts, high summer brimming like a tide.

Swiftly the summer days blended into one another.

Heat throbbed like a great anvil, and hot glassy air shimmered over the dusty-smelling corn. Or a burst of rain would come, in a great glistening mesh. Nights were vast and fragrant with wind and stars and the wavering sound of far frogs. Weariness, like armor, over their bodies, Jim and Anna would sit in the blue night; Anna, her head against the top step of the porch, caressing the flowers in her lap as if they were about to vanish; Jim, puffing a pipe, trying to empty his mind, keep it motionless on the *now,* not on the past or what might come. The breath of the moon, mist and silver, lay on the fields; the flowers clustered in bright shadows in the darkness. After a long while Anna would laugh, a strange mirthless laugh, and rise to go into the house. Then Jim too would follow, knocking the ashes out of his pipe onto the vine, giving a last broad look over the night and the earth. Sometimes seeing them sit so in the night, a sharp unhappiness would pierce the golden haze in Mazie's heart; but the blur of days descending so swiftly would wash it out again.

Once, hungry, degraded, after a beating from Anna for some mischief, Mazie lay by the roadside, bedded in the clover, belly down, feeling the earth push back against her, feeling the patterns of clover smell twine into her nostrils till she was drugged with the scent. The soft plodding of a buggy gathered into her consciousness.

She turned on her back. Above the stars clustered, low, bright, still-winged. As if she had never seen them before. Her breath caught. The buggy was stopping, and an old man got out. Old Man Caldwell.

"Lost?" he breathed softly in the soft night.

"No, just watchin the stars. I live in that house over there—Holbrook's house. My name's Mazie Holbrook."

He came over and lay down beside her, so quiet in the dimness he did not seem to be there. He was looking up too, making it a trusting dark.

"Stars," she began, "what are they now? Splinters offn the moon I've heard it said. But more likely they're lamps in houses up there, or flowers growin in the night. I'd like to smell the smell that would be comin offn those flowers."

He raised up on his elbow, staring at her. Then said, "Stars are suns. Like our sun. But so far away—so many miles no one can imagine—they look tiny."

"You know them things? Then what is the sun, a fire?"

"Miles of fire, many times bigger than the earth. But more than fire."

"Yes, a fire. Now I know, I can see that the stars are fire, for they are dancing now like a fire movin."

He laughed. Then told her why the stars seemed dancing, how old stars were, how they lived and died, and of a people living long ago, the Greeks, who had named these stars and had found in their shapes images of what was on earth below. As his words misted into the night and disappeared, she scarcely listened—only the aura over them of timelessness, of vastness, of eternal things that had been before her and would be after her, remained and entered into her with a great hurt and wanting.

Hot midsummer nights when the bedroom of sweating, tossing bodies was too much for her, she would slip out into the fields and the sad hurt would gather into her again, seeing an old old people lying in just such a field, tracing out names and images in the heavens where splashes of enormous fire whirled, eternal and timeless, and tangled comets hissed.

One day, coming in because the hot dust pricked her feet so, she saw him again, sitting with Ben on his lap, watching Anna put up tomato preserve. He was saying, "Vultures running it now. It doesn't make any difference whether it's republican or democrat; the same hand pulls the strings." She was going to ask him what he meant, but Anna answered into the kettle of steaming tomatoes, "The bellwether leads the flock all right, but who is it sees they're led how he wants? The one that trains the bellwether."

"Exactly . . . When I came out, a man had some chance. The only thing against him was nature, locusts and drought and late frost. You took your chances. That was all you had to fight. But now that hardly matters. There's mortgage, taxes, the newest kind of machinery to buy so you do as good as the next fellow, and the worry—will it get a price this year."

Anna stopped stirring, straightened up, steam or sweat beaded on her intense face. "In college did you learn why all that is?"

"In college . . ." He choked off his words and his face went frozen. "My education began after I got out of college." Then seeing Mazie, "Hello my star-gazing companion . . . Mrs. Holbrook, children have marvelous minds. I hate to see what life does to 'em."

Fall came. A dribble of gaudy leaves over the roads. Sheets of taffeta-gold corn brimming the fields. Days alive with the throb of the threshing machine and the low moo of cows calling across the meadows. Under the full moon, the kids sang and played hide-go-seek in the hay, or listened to hear the apple trees plop their fruit upon the ground.

School began. Mazie and Will went for the first time. The playground squirming with kids was wonderful, but the teacher that waddled and held her head like a duck, and her wheezing horror—"Eight years old and can't read yet, you'll have to go in the first grade with your brother Will"—was shame. Yet the lessons came easy—the crooked white worms of words on the second-grade blackboard magically transforming into words known and said, although they were still stumbling over the first-grade alphabet. Finding the two could suddenly read, the teacher put them both up one grade, but the primer already breathlessly raced through with only silly sentences as a reward, they spent most of their time listening secretly to the upper grades recite jography and history—far countries, strange peoples.

Anna's face would glow. "What did you learn today?" And Mazie would try to tell her. "See Jim," she would say, handing Mazie or Will a catalogue, hearing them stumble through the words, "see? they're reading. They'll be something, these kids."

For the first time, Mazie was acutely conscious of her scuffed shoes, rag-bag clothes, quilt coat. Stripping corn, she kept the soft silk; buried in the hay, she would dream of somehow weaving it into garments incredible. But the tassels withered, grew brown and smelly, and she had to throw them away. Sometimes, when the sadness in her heart became intolerable, she gathered Will and Ben and baby Jim about her and recited for them a poem learned from Old Man Caldwell. Not in his chaffing tones, but in a deep mysterious voice:

O Were I a Lum Ti Tum Tum
In the land of the alivoo fig
I'd play on the strum ti tum tum
To the tune of the thinguma jig.

Here, her voice would ripen into tragedy:

And if in the Lum Ti Tums battle I fall
A thingamys all that I crave
Oh bury me deep in the whatcha may call
And plant thingumbobs over my grave.

Reciting it, the sadness would ebb; the autumn world became blue and gold again.

One autumn dusk, with the calling of birds making her restless and a great gilt sunset clotting over the prairie, Mazie left the smoky kitchen and ran down the road. There was something to escape from. The autumn air, sweet with mellow death. But more, something in the kitchen; her father with anger riding on his brow, the shadow curtaining her mother's eyes. Momma'll hit me for runnin way thout doing the dishes, she thought, but a hunger and fear pushed her forward.

There was a great star glowing in the heart of the sunset, like a still candle in a vast unmoving flame. She could feel its glow on her face. As it sank, she began to run across the fields, to follow it; the corn stubble cut into her bare feet, but she knew only the sky dimming, the great star pulling down over the horizon, into the night, and something vanishing with it. Then it was gone, only darkness left, standing very tall and black about her.

With a bite of agony, she felt the slashes in her feet. Whimpering softly, a great void swelling in her, she started to find the road. Up ahead a big quiet hulk loomed, with a sultry light in one window. Caldwell's house, she thought; that must be Caldwell's house.

Bess Ellis answered the door. "Why, Mazie! What's brought you all the way up here?"

"I . . ." Her feet made a silent screaming. "I come to borry a book or a catalogue for to read."

Bess opened her mouth to say something, then closed it again. "Well, come in. Dad's pretty sick, I guess you know; but he'll be glad to see you."

Mazie walked into the light; stared incredulous. There was a gleaming sink and a great white cabinet. Upon the table, on a white tablecloth, glowed a bowl of vegetables bursting with snow cabbage and crimson tomatoes and hard round radishes. In the other room she could see a white plaster head and a wall of books.

Blood dribbled from her feet onto the kitchen linoleum; guiltily she forbade herself to notice. Bess was calling from the other room, "Come on into Dad's room—he wants to see you." He lay in the bed, curiously withered. Unmoving, only his eyes alive. Mazie took a step backward.

His fragile voice shattered about her. "Come by the bed, child." His hand, only a shadow of weight, embraced her shoulder. "I'm glad you came, Mazie. I think about you. How is your mother?"

She did not know what to say. A fear hovered. Outside the window there was still a faint light low in the west, like vanishing wings of birds. She fastened her eyes there. He kept on talking.

"Tell her to come see me, your mother. You remember what you thought the stars were, Mazie, before I told you?"

She nodded.

"Splinters of the moon, you said. Or maybe flowers in the night. Keep that wondering, Mazie, but try to *know*. Build on the knowing with the wondering. Mazie . . ."

She had to turn her eyes to him. His head was moving from side to side as if something were caught choking in his throat.

"Mazie. Live, don't exist. Learn from your mother, who has had everything to grind out life and yet has kept life. Alive, felt what's real, known what's real. People can live their whole life not knowing."

The words were incomprehensible. They parched the fear, but thirstily she still watched his eyes.

"You don't know how few . . . 'Better,' your mother says, 'to be a cripple and alive than dead, not able to feel anything.' But there is more—to rebel against what will not let life be. Your mother thought to move from the mine to the farm would be enough, but . . ."

The hand was suddenly heavy on her shoulder. He raised himself.

An old man, Elias Caldwell, death already smothering his breast, tries to tell a child something of all he has learned, something of what he would have her live by—and hears only incoherent words come out. Yet the thoughts revolve, revolve and whirl, a scorching nebula in his breast, sending forth flaming suns that only shatter against the walls and return to chaos. How can it be said? Once I lived in softness and ease and sickened. Once I chose a stern life, turning to people hard, bitter and strong—obscure people, the smell of soil and sweat about them—the smell of life . . .

But I failed. I brought them nothing. To die, how bitter when nothing was done with my life. And the nebula whirls and revolves, sending its scorching suns that break in a chaos of inarticulateness about this child with a sound of fear. Nothing of it said.

His voice goes on. "Whatever happens, remember, everything, the nourishment, the roots you need, are where you are now."

The voice falters, dies; *no, none of it can be said when I myself do . . . not . . . know.*

She sits with a sense of non-being over her—of someone other than she sitting there timeless, suspended in a dusky room, a voice gathering around her; kind still hands of sound flaring into words meaningless and strange, meaningless when one tries to understand, but meaningful for a fleeting second. And she creeps her hand over the hand that lies on her shoulder. He laughs. A musical grieving sound. Calling, "Bess, see she gets some of the books. Those fairy tales, Wilde's, and the Dickens and Blake, and that book of Greek myths. Someday she will read them.

"Goodbye my wonder-gazer companion."

Whimpering, running down the road, each step pain, the shadows were long and clutched at her, the corn by the wayside, some fallen, some shorn, was desolate and terrible, a flesh of her flesh.

Coming to the kitchen, she heard her father's angry voice: "They're taking all of it, every damn thing. The whole year slaved to nothing. I owe *them*—some joke if it wasnt so bloody—I owin *them* after workin like a team of mules for a year. They're wantin the cow and

Nellie . . . takin Fred Benson's farm and Eldridge's. Batten on us like hogs. The bastards. A whole year— now I'm owin them."

The wind started a laughter in the fallen dead leaves, stirred them round and round senselessly in a mocking mimicry of being alive, beat its mocking laughter through the trees up over the sky.

Caldwell died a week later. Mazie never got the books—Jim sold them for half a dollar when he got to town, though Anna cursed him for it. As for Mazie's slashed feet, it was weeks before she could do without rag bandages, could bear the wearing of shoes.

Overnight in late October, the ground grew hard and unyielding. Mazie and Will, trudging to school, felt their blood draw into little lumps under their skin and congeal under the touch of the wind. Tears would be frozen down their faces by the time they reached the schoolhouse, and Willie's feet, in their torn shoes, insensible. The snow came and fastened itself upon the earth. Finally it lay in too high waves of white over the fields, so that Mazie and Will had to stay home. Then the school itself closed.

Days were dim and short. Snow lay on the earth continually—blinding white at noon, yellow and old at dusk, ghost white at night. Life ceased beyond the kitchen. In the circle of warmth around the stove, everything moved and revolved. Distance was enormously magnified by the cold. Far and far it seemed to the woodpile; to the henhouse, where the hens gathered in drooping ovals of dejection, their cheeps coming out in little frozen spears; to the stable, where the sweet rotting smell of hay and the great cloud of warm breath from the cow stained the air. They scarcely moved from the stove. All day they sat around, Will's staccato cough mingling with Baby Jim's ceaseless sniffling. Anna was pregnant again—caught in the drowse of it, drugged by the warmth, she let things be. In the yellow kerosene light at night, she sewed or thumbed over the pages of a catalogue. But the other work she left. Dirty clothes gathered into a waiting pile, bacon drippings coiled greasy in the bottom of the pans, bread went unmade, and the smell of drying diapers layered over the room. Meals were quick, slapped together, half burned. It drove Jim crazy. The untidiness, the closeness, the inaction. The querulous children, half sick, always hungry—thinning, while Anna grew monstrous fat as if she were feeding on them.

"A woman's goddamn life," he would shout, "sittin around huggin a stove." Then contrite, jerk out long fiery stories to the kids, sometimes stopping abruptly in the middle to brood. He whittled toys for them— blocks, dolls, animals, and gentle with Anna, straightened up for her, kneaded the bread. But when it was time for the chores, for the first time he would be eager, alert.

Quarrels flared up. Sometimes he beat up on the kids. Anna, the dream paralysis on her, unlike her old self, scarcely seemed to hear or care. "Snowed in like this leaves a man too much with himself," Jim would explain. "He starts askin why, and what for, like a kid."

One day through the sad sifting sound of snow came the high cheep of newborn chicks. Jim ran out. "Some fool hen hiding her eggs and settin. Wonder she didn't pick out the ice on the crick to set on. C'mon, Mazie."

He piled chicks into her apron. Very alive and vital she felt in all the frozen world, but inside the house again, with a tiny oval of fluff against her cheek, barely moving, a shadow of sorrow fell on her heart. They put the chicks in the oven to warm, and Jim disappeared— probably to plow through the snow to a neighbor's for drink and talk.

The afternoon was a short gray blur; whirring of white against the windows, and stillness, except for the crackling of icicles and the short quick *spfft* of wood in the stove. Nobody noticed when the cheep became hysterical, and finally ceased. Mazie and Ben peopled a city with things cut out of a catalogue, while Will watched them, his head a tangle of fever, remembering how the snow had soaked through his shoddy shoes and he could not be out till spring. Anna sat unmoving by the stove, her hands over her belly, a half smile of wisdom on her mouth, coming out of her dream to say, "Wipe Jim's nose, Mazie. I see the grease didn't do no good to drive that cough out, Will." And then sinking back into the dream again.

Jim came in. He stood at the door a moment, blind. For the first time, they noticed the smell of burning. "Criszake." He swung to the oven in one step and opened it. "The chicks, sure enough. Roasted to death. Have I got a bunch of dummies in here that can't even smell?"

No one answered. With shocked eyes, they stared. "Dumb, too? Your mouths stuffed up like your noses with crap? But you'll smell 'em." He grabbed Anna and forced her down by the open oven. "You'll fill your eyes with 'em."

She flung herself free. "Don't touch me."

"Don't touch ya, huh. You don't always talk like

that. No wonder I never got anywhere. No wonder nothing ever comes right. Lots of help I get from my woman."

"You get plenty help. Kitchen help, farm help, milkin help, washwoman help. And motherin too."

"Who asked for your goddamn brats?"

"Who? I'll never have another, to starve to death with you."

"No wonder we're starvin. Look at the woman I got."

"Poppa, stop, Momma, don't," Ben was screaming. Mazie held Jim scooped in her arms, her head buried in his baby body to stifle the sounds. Only Will moved. He was pulling on his father's pants leg, shouting, "Don't, don't, don't."

"Oh, fine bargains you make, fine bargains," Anna taunted. "Anybody can cheat you out of anything. Can't even make a livin. Fine bargains—how to starve your wife and kids quickest."

"Shut up."

"Oh sure, it was all goin to be fine. A new life, and you made one all right. A new way to keep us cold and wanting."

"*Shut up.*" His fist crashed against her shoulder; she sagged under it. For a moment he stared at her, at the crying children, at Will beating him with small fists, at the diapers flapping over the stove, then he went out the door, closing it behind him, dark.

The worst storm in years arose that night. Over the torn and scattered sky, a wild hungry darkness came; then snow, driving in the wind like steel whips. The window in the bedroom shattered on the floor before it, and neither the chair bottom pounded over, or the quilts stuffed around, kept the bitterness out. For three nights they all slept on a mattress on the kitchen floor, Mazie and Anna venturing out only twice a day with a bucket of hot coals to warm their hands over when they milked the cow or fed the horse and hog. The chickens they brought to the cellar and bedded in straw.

Outside, the charred bodies of the chicks lay where Anna had thrown them. That night, the snow covered. Four days later the sun rose at last, over a vast white world pure and unmoving.

It was ten days before Jim returned. Where he went or what he did, he never told.

Early in March, Mazie and Will wandered to a high wood where hidden wild violets with tears in their eyes carpeted the ground. Restless, Mazie pressed herself into the earth, but the soft dankness brought a faint remembrance of a face like jelly pushed against hers. Shuddering, she got up again. "Butterflies live behind your eyes, Will, butterflies. Their wings all colored. You dont believe me? Go ahead and try it—push your finger in your eye and you'll see 'em, butterfly wings."

Ugly and ugly the earth. Patches of soiled snow oozing away, leaving the ground like great dirty sores between; scabs of old leaves that like a bruise hid the violets underneath. Trees fat with oily buds, and the swollen breasts of prairie. Ugly. She turned her eyes to the sky for oblivion, but it was bellies, swollen bellies, black and corpse gray, puffing out baggier and baggier, cloud belly on cloud belly till at the zenith they pushed vast and swollen. Her mother. Night, sweating bodies. The blood and pain of birth. Nausea groveled. "Think I'm lyin, just push your finger in your eyes and you'll

see. Butterflies." She could feel words swollen big
within her, words coming out with pain, bloody, all
clothed in red. She began to hit Will, hard, ferocious.
Then a weakness of tears—"Wouldja live in a room all
breath, all winter breath?" He was raining small futile
blows on her, blows unfelt. "Oh Will, Oh were I a Lum
Ti Tum Tum." Ugly. Swollen like bellies.

She wakened that night to a nightmare of Jim's savage hand on her shoulder. "Wake up now. Your
mother's goin to have a baby, and you've got to help
her. I'm drivin over to Ellis's and takin Will and Ben.
You put on water for me, now, right away."

The nausea came again. In the kitchen her mother
was sitting, on her face a look of not seeing, although
the black gates of her eyes opened on something too
far to see to.

"Momma," Mazie cried, frightened, pressing her
head in her mother's knees. "Momma."

For a moment Anna turned her eyes to her, with a
look compassionate and troubled. "It's allright Mazie.
I'm beginnin to have the baby; it's my time. I told
Poppa not to leave you." Her face masked into a
stranger's again, and her body stiffened, her hand
clutching the chair back. Spacing her words she said,
"Better fire up the stove. Then come in the bedroom
and help me fix up the bed."

The blackened fire leapt under her touch to embers
and later to flame. Cheerlessly the water fled into the
bucket and teakettle. But there was still the bedroom to
be faced. She found her mother quietly kneeling before
a drawer, holding a sheet. "Here," she said in a remote
voice, "we'll put this one on. Then get out those newspapers."

"Yes, Momma." A nausea was gathering into her
breast, clotting there. "Yes."

They came at last so that she could flee into the night. But the clatter of their voices came after. Uneven words. She clutched herself and sank into the soft dust. A forlorn wind fingered her hair and went gently over her body. But the nausea contested there, unmoving. Yes, Momma. The face set like a mask, purified, austere. To fix her mind to a time of dancing when laughter rose like froth; but the face curtained over everything. Yes, Momma. Mis' Burgum was saying something about a dry birth, the waters broke. She crept into the henhouse, not to hear. Full and quiet in the darkness the house lay, and the fields beyond.

Then, strangely, hunger came. Trickles of it in her mouth, battling under the nausea. Food—the smell of it yearned in her nostrils. She found an egg, warm. It slipped down her throat, then it was washing up again, spurting over the ground. Yes Momma. I'm sick, Momma. Butterflies lives behind your eyes. Perhaps there were stars above, known stars. Light, weightless, she walked out to the yard, the earth under her feet like air, and turned her face to the heavens. Pale, half drowned, blurred like through tears: the stars. Where was the belted man Caldwell had told her of, lifting his shield against a horn of stars? Where was the bright one she had run after into the sunset? A strange face, the sky grieved above her, gone suddenly strange like her mother's.

After a long while she felt a drenching mist. Rain, she thought without thinking. A shadow of rain. Back in the henhouse, she heard it descend upon the earth, gentle and grieving. Perhaps after a while she slept, a half sleep into which voices came. "Now. Push hard now, Anna. Did you boil the spoon? I have to use it. Hard, Anna."

Then a cry, ecstatic, profound, shattered the night,

and a thin wail wove it under. It was dawn. Her father's arms were carrying her into the house through the gray and lonely light, his voice saying "looked . . . so long. You tired Bigeyes? . . . I had to leave you in the rain. . . ."

The sleep still lay on her, or was it sleeplessness. Yellow light flowered before her in the warmth of the kitchen. "Her breasts cracked so it'll be no fun feedin the youngun," someone was saying, and "where'd you find her, Jim?"

Bess cradled her. "You really set on leaving, Jim?"

"You know it's no use to stay."

"But what if you cant get on at the slaughterhouse?"

"I'm goin anyhow. Soon as Anna's fit to. We cant stay here."

"Things wont be better other places, Jim. How can they? . . . You go to sleep now, Mazie. Everything's all right."

"They cant be worse. Anyway, I've got to try."

"Life," heavily from Ellen Burgum. "Life's no bottle of perfume. I'm tired enough to die."

Two figures moving with pain in the dawn darkness, in the vapor mist. Two voices lashed by a dry and savage wind, bringing strangely the scent of lilac.

"Almost time now, Anna. We'd better go."

"Yes. It's so quiet now, Jim."

"Mr. Burgum's waiting."

"You'd think you could hear somebody's rooster. Doesnt seem like other mornin's we woke up to work in."

"No. C'mon, Anna. Let's go. Now."

"Funny how Will cried all last night, and Mazie wouldn't sleep but in the hay. You'd think children wouldn't care."

"Anna—they're waiting."

"This hay smells good. I'd like to breathe it in so's not ever to forget."

"Right away now, or we'll miss the train."

"Right away now, Jim. . . . Jim, what's the matter, life never lets anything be? . . . Just a year ago . . . I tried for us to have a good life. You tried too, Jim."

One word, austere. "Anna."

Two figures blur into one, gnarled and lonely. Very low he says: "You're shivering. Cold?"

"Awful cold. Lets go. Now."

"But you cant take it lying down—like a dog. You just cant, Anna."

FIVE

Myriad and drumming, the feet of sound move always through these crooked streets, trembling the shoddy houses, jerking the skeleton children who scream and laugh so senselessly to uneven rhythms they themselves know not of. Monster trucks shake by, streetcars plunge, machinery rasps and shrieks. Far underneath thinly quiver the human noises—weeping and scolding and tired words that slip out in monosyllables and are as if never spoken; sighs of lust, and guttural, the sigh of weariness; laughter sometimes, but this sound can scarcely be called human, not even in the mouths of children. A fog of stink smothers down over it all—so solid, so impenetrable, no other smell lives beside it. Human smells, crotch and underarm sweat, the smell of cooking or of burning, all are drowned under, merged into the vast unmoving stench.

That stench is a reminder—a proclamation—*I rule here*. It speaks for the packing houses, heart of all that moves in these streets; gigantic heart—pumping over the artery of viaducts the men and women who are the streets' lifeblood, nourishing the taverns and brothels and rheumy-eyed stores, bulging out the soiled and exhausted houses, and multiplying into these children playing so mirthlessly in their street yards where flower only lampposts. (They say this heart pumps lifeblood

far and far—thin and blue the vein—to purest air
where scents flower under glass and in hundred-dollar
perfume bottles, and a rare and cherished few are
nourished.

A man's face, heavy and sullen (strange and bright
the blue of his eyes) moves here awhile and is gone:
Jim; a woman's face, thinning, skin tightening over the
broad cheekbones, the great dark eyes down a terrace
of sunken flesh, fading until the eyelids shut over forever: *Anna.* A child's thin face looks up a moment,
wondering dazed eyes: *Mazie;* a boy's face, scowl over
the mouth, eyes hurt with the hurt of not understanding,
then insane with anger; *Will.* On this face, half baby's,
half child's, the breath of fever glows, closing the
sober eyes; a tiny boy running along croons a song that
is silenced; a tiny girl's fists beat the air, stiffening,
stiffened: *Ben, Jimmie, Baby Bess.*

Yes, it is here Jim and Anna Holbrook have come to
live. (Old and familiar the streets to them, the scenery
of their childhood, rearranged.) Over the cobbled
streets, past the two blocks of dump and straggling
grass, past the human dumpheap where the nameless
FrankLloydWrights of the proletariat have wrought
their wondrous futuristic structures of flat battered tin
cans, fruit boxes and gunny sacks, cardboard and
mother earth. In this ancient battered house that leans
toward the river. What matter the second story, windowless and roofless, the paper-thin boards, the dirt
which has eaten into and become a part of the walls?
It has a space that might be called a yard, and when
the wind blows hard to the west, you can smell river
and dump instead of packing house.

(And Beauty? Until the mammoth stone beauty of
the city has carved itself into their blood, the children
can lie on their bellies near the edge of the cliff and

watch the trains and freights, the glittering railroad tracks, the broken bottles dumped below, the rubbish moving on the littered belly of the river.)

"See, Anna," says Jim. "It's got a yard for the kids. They wont be runnin out in the streets to play, anyhow. And just think, runnin water with a faucet and a toilet inside the house. We never had that before."

"No" (trying not to see or smell).

"And electric lights. Hey, over there, kids—you ever see electric lights in the house? and electric lights if we want."

"If we want?"

"You know what I mean, if we can fork over. We'll have 'em too, quickern a hen could lay an egg."

"Yes. Lets go inside, Jim." (Holding Baby Bess to her nostrils, holding Bess against the corrosive eating into her heart.)

"Sure—and four rooms. Say, what's the matter with you? lookin as if you're seein a corpse. I know this aint no palace, but you ought to see what other folks are livin in for what we're paying."

"Sure Jim, I know it's a real find. Guess I'm tired, that's all."

"Ma," said Ben, running up, "what smells so awful funny? It makes me sick to my tummy, Ma. It smell like this all the time?"

When Anna made Will and Mazie ready for school that first morning, she stood them up against the wall and said fiercely, "You two got a chance to really learn something now; you're goin to a good school, not a country one. I catch you not doin good and I'll knock the livin daylights out of you, you hear?"

But Mazie hated it. The first day: "MazieandWill-

Holbrookhavecomefromthecountrywheretheygrowthe-
cornandwheatandallourmilkcomesfromsayhellotoMazie
andWillchildren." Her palm held in Will's moist with
fear. A big room, biggern the whole country school,
squirming with faces, staring. ("Whatcha shiverin for,
you scairt?" "Me? Scared?") Faces mad and tired and
scared and hungry and dead and their eyes like they
want to eat you up. No, dont look at the faces, look
out the window—but it is greasy, like drippings was
smeared all over, and stink comes in from the top,
comes in and fills the room. All the faces (if her heart
wouldn't beat so fast) . . . Dont look, read the funny
words on the blackboard—Na-tion-al-it-ies American
Armenian Bohemian Chinese Croatian (Croation—
that was what ol' man Kvaternick was, ol' man Kvaternick in the mine and he was dead now, dead. Worms
. . . no dont think of ol' man Kvaternick) Irish French
Italian Jewish Lith . . . A face was black, black like
when the men come up from the mine; lots of faces
were black. Maybe the mine was here in the city too,
maybe kids had to live in the mine like they had to
live in gunnysack houses, maybe the whistle would
be again, but the whistle was all the time here. Mexican
Negro Polish Portuguese. If her heart beat any faster
she would have to scream and all the faces would turn
and look, . . . One face was honey color—honey like
on the farm. The farm. It is just a dream, a bad
dream, and it really is the farm, really the farm, in a
minute now you will get awake, and it will be the
farm again.

At recess, her heart quieting, telling two girls, Annamae and Ellie, about riding a horse, somebody hissed:
"So ya come from the country where our milk comes
from; ya learn about bulls?" and smack, a head butted

her in the stomach. Bewildered, gasping for breath, swaying, she heard Annamae laugh, "Oh, Smoky, didja put that one over," and in a darkness of rage and hatred she lunged at him, but already he was across the playground, his too big shirt flapping in the wind, his angular face jeering. And then she turned to Ellie and shoved her down, and turned to Annamae to shove her down, but the teacher was holding her shoulder, steering her inside the school. "Perhaps you indulged in rough play of this nature where you came from, but we do not permit it here, nor does it go unpunished." Mazie could still see Smoky's jeering face. "Lemme alone," she cried and, making her body a hard ball of force, wrenched herself free. Then, paralyzed at what she had done she stood in front of them all and began to cry. Hearing Will savagely whisper to someone next to him, "That aint my sister, that aint my sister" she cried louder and louder, uncontrollably.

That night they went to the Bedners, old friends Jim and Anna hadn't seen for seven years. Alex was doing well—he was a tool and die maker now. They lived in a five-room house with a piano and a stained-glass window, and it didn't smell around there, except when the wind blew strong from the south. They went on a streetcar, the kids' first ride, but only Will seemed jubilant. Jimmie and Bess slept, Ben was sick all the way, and Mazie kept looking out the window with her eyes shut tight. Anna, kept smoothing her hair and passing her hand over the lines in her face.

Else let out a cry of pain when she saw her: "Why, Anna, honey, you've changed so, I wouldn't hardly've known you."

"But a lot happens in seven years," Anna reminded her.

"So it does, so it does," Else agreed and began to cry. She was fat and smelled too sweet and had on a tight yellow dress. "So you're Anna's little man," she said to Will, tears still on her face. "Give an old friend a kiss." But Will wouldn't. He ran over to the piano and banged it, and Jim had to slap him before he would kiss her.

Everything was strained and shaken. Jimmie and Will ran into the other rooms to watch the electric lights on the ceiling and turn them on and off. Alex cleared his throat, then Jim cleared his, and then they smoked cigars in silence. In a low voice Else was saying to Anna, "So stuck up around here . . . So lonesome I could die . . . such a brood . . . and we cant even manage to get one . . . been to all the doctors . . . just breaks my heart . . ."

On a little table there were a lot of magazines. *Screen Star* and *True Confession*. Mazie turned the pages—there were pictures in them of men and ladies smiling, or kissing. Alex, his thumb in his lapel, his voice suddenly loud and important, said, "Now if you still cant get on by the end of the week at the yards, you go on down and see Mulcahey; he's the biggest contractor in town for road and sewer work—and he dont hire niggers or furriners when there's white men begging."

"O.K.," said Jim, but he looked awfully funny.

"Well, believe me," Alex said, noting that look, "a man cant pick and choose nowadays."

"He cant pick and choose," said Jim, "but he can sure pick and shovel."

Nobody laughed but Else, who laughed and laughed for a long time. "You grow up with your papa's sense of humor," she said to Ben, curled up in her lap, "and you'll have them in the aisles. My, but he's a cute tyke,

Annie. Who woulda thought Mazie would grow up to be so homely? She was such a cunning baby. But they do say a homely kid makes a pretty girl."

Mazie pretended not to hear. "Who plays the piano?" she asked as loud as she could.

"Me, honey, if you can stand plunking. Your ma used to play real good by ear. Why dont you play something for us now, honey?"

Mazie thought her mother was going to have another sinking spell, she looked so awful. But her voice sounded all right. "I haven't touched the piano since I don't know when," she said. "*You* play, Else."

Else sat down on the piano bench. As she played she swayed her body. Underneath her dress you could see her flesh ripple. But when she began to sing, Jimmie came from the other room and put his head up against her lap, and Will came in too and stood listening. Alex began to sing, and then Jim and Anna. One after another they sang old songs, some Jim or sometimes Anna had sung in old times of happiness; some the children had never heard before. "Red River Valley," "Sweet Genevieve," "When It's Lamplighting Time," "In the Gloaming," "When You and I Were Young, Maggie," "The Wreck of the Old '91," "Down in the Valley," "Roamin' So Far," "Shenandoah," "Nelly Gray," Foster songs, "I Saw a Ship A-Sailing."

From the opened window, the sweet intoxicating smell of spring floated in; the lamplight made soft lakes of light, shadows bending over, gentle. They sang and sang, and a longing, a want undefined, for something lost, for something never known, troubled them all. The separate voices chorded into one great full one, their faces into beauty. Oh, singin is like . . . Mazie, broken, searched for the word, feeling tears stand be-

hind her eyelids. Singin is like . . . But no right
words would come. Bess, quietly sleeping, wore an
eternal dream look. Singing one of Anna's favorite
song:

Throw your arms round me, 'fore it's too late
Throw your arms round me, feel my heart break

a fifth voice, pure, ethereal, veiled over the rest. Mazie
saw it was Jimmie, crouched at the pedals of the piano.
"Ma," she said after the song was done, "it's Jimmie,
JimJim was singin too." Incredulous, they made him
sing it over with them and over and over. His words
were a blur, a shadow of the real words, but the mel-
ody came true and clear.

And then it was over. Else, the same chirp, the
dearie and honey, the perspiration rings under her arm,
Alex laughing too loud, and Jim trying too hard to
laugh, and Anna sitting shrunken and ill, her arm tenderly around Jimmie.

The weariness. The ghastly nausea in her belly (in
all their bellies) from the stench. Ben feverish in bed
with it. And her banner of defiance—up the first
day—the clean cheesecloth curtains, yellowing, browning. All that scrubbing to make a whiteness inside—
and the stubborn walls and floors only a deeper smoke
color. Even the cardboard tacked for a carpet in the
front room so Jimmie crawling around would cease to
be a graveyard for splinters—even that was damp and
soggy and would have to be ripped up again. How the
house resisted her.

Anna sat in the armless chair, Bess tugging at her
breast and pulling away and tugging again and giving

out small frantic cries. "Guzzle, kitten, guzzle, dont make such a fuss." All that scrubbing and she was always so tired nowadays. So awfully tired. "C'mon, Bessie, hold still and eat." Well, she'd try washing soda in the scrubbing water next time. Maybe that might do the trick.

A fine joke on Jim to be back in the earth again, sewering. He should've known the stockyards job couldn't pan out in spring when they were laying off. How they'd ever manage on what he was getting with the rent high as it was and the children needing this and that. Awful to be sendin them to school looking like they did. And Will wouldn't mind anymore, as if he knew . . .

A familiar faintness dizzied her. With Bess still crying and tugging she sank to the bed, thinking: I oughta see what Jimmie's doin and set him down on the hopper. But she was wandering through old childhood streets. Bess lay in the scrub pail, under water. And Jim was fleeing, shrinking to a tiny dot on the lurid sky. A speck of dust floated from where he had gone, growing larger. And now the gaunt haggard house towered above. Where were the children? MazieWillBen she cried, but a smell was filling her mouth so no words could come. "It'll fall," she tried desperately to warn, beating it away with her broom. Right in front of her, right to the house, Will danced. "It'll crash," she screamed. It crashed. "Momma, Momma," someone was calling. "Yes, Ben," she managed to answer, "I'm coming." She had to steady herself against the wall, her body drenched with sweat and fear. The dizziness was still there. Funny how Bess was sleeping, still sucking away as if she had the nipple in her mouth.

Outside a wan sunshine lay over the grimy streets, the streets of her dream. She pulled the blinds down. Will was sitting in the kitchen morose, just home from school, chewing bread with drippings on it. "Didnt you hear your brother callin?" Anna asked. "Dont you know he's sick?" He just looked back at her, not answering. "All right, git in there with this drink of water afore I skin you alive." There, her head felt better now, the splashing water cooling her cheeks.

The little stream on the farm glinted in the sun of her memory, and Mazie was spraying her with water, laughing. That was gone, it was long ago, it was forgotten.

"Well, you little horntoad, now what's the matter, waking your momma up first chance today she's had to get a little rest."

"I can't breav, Momma." (You'd think he'd get used to the smell in two weeks.)

"Sure you can, see you're breathin now, you've been breathing all the time; here, we'll make a bundle and prop it under your head."

"No Momma, cant breav . . . Let's go home, Momma. It smells of vomit here. I had a dream and Shep was barkin for me, tellin me not to smell vomit no more, and come back to the farm. It's so hard to breav. It smells so hot, so awful hot."

(The farm—why couldnt the kids leave her alone about it?) And what was the matter with Will? Looking at her face like that and now hitting Ben, shouting, "Shut up, you crybaby, you big crybaby, shut up or I'll kill ya." And she was holding Will and hitting him. "What did you do that for?" beating him till she sank to her knees, still drenched in sweat, trembling from nervousness and crying, and Ben was out of bed with great sober eyes, stroking her cheek, begging, "Dont cry Momma, don't cry," and outside Will was shouting to Mazie, "Does too smell like vomit, worse'n vomit, worse'n dead dogs and garbage, worse'n the crap can. I'm gonna run away to the farm, you come too, Mazie," and Mazie was yelling back, "Shut up, we are on the farm, we are on the farm," and Will was quiet suddenly, asking of the sky, "What's the matter with everything anyhow?" and running, running down the street. And in the front room, Jimmie pounding on the wall was yelling, "Out, out. Lemme out. Out."

Into her great physical pain and weariness Anna stumbled and lost herself. Remote she fed and clothed the children, scrubbed, gave herself to Jim, clenching her fists against a pain she had no strength to feel. In the front room Jimmie played and sang to himself, falling asleep when she didn't come for him, wetting his overalls when she forgot. Else worried over her: "Land sake, Anna, what's the matter with you anyhow? You useta be strong as a bull, and look at you now. You aint even ornery with the kids. You take this here tonic now, you hear? It'll do you good. It says for all female complaints."

"All female complaints, huh?" Anna answered. "Well, I guess I got all of them. But I never was much of a hand at patent medicines." On the kitchen shelf, the bottle mantled in dust.

Bess shrank and yellowed. Anna fussed with food. "You really think Eagle Brand is good, Mis' Kryckszi? It oughta be the way they soak you for it, but you never can tell. And Bess needs perkin up bad. When it's tomato season, I'll try juice, they say that's awful good. But when I gave her some of what I'd canned on the farm, she spit it right back. And just look how she's gettin blue around the mouth and squalls all the time now."

But she could not really care. Only sometimes, nursing the baby, chafing the little hands to warm them, old songs would start from her lips and tears well from her eyes, tears she did not even know she was weeping, till Ben would come in, standing lacerated till she would notice him and ask, "What's the matter, Benjy, did you hurt yourself?" and he could come over to her and say gently, "Mommy, you're crying."

The money going drove Jim crazy. "Jesus Christ, woman," he would shout, "where does it all go to? God knows we're eatin worse'n animals, and Bess eatin off you dont cost no more. You useto be so smart with money—make it stretch like rubber. Now it's rent week and not a red cent in the house. I tell you we gotta make what I'm gettin do—they're takin off for my waterproofs."

But she could not heed—the old Anna of sharp words and bitter exaction, and fierce attempt to make security for her children was gone, lost in a fog of pain that seemed the only reality. Will was the only one that really saw—but a lust for the streets was on him, a lust to hit back, a lust not to care. He had learned how to scramble up and down the cliff, hanging onto roots and digging his toes into the crumbling clay; he knew the railroad tracks and the walk and talk of the bindle stiffs hightailing it down the roadbed; he knew the dump and the kids on his block and strange wild games to play. And in these, in the quick movements of his body, for a while he anesthetized himself.

Ben saw too—but in the confused, entangled way of a small child whose mind is a prism through which the light shatters into a thousand gleams and shadows that can never come whole. Say rather, a weight, an oppression dragged always in his chest; a darkening shadow hovered over his days that in moments descended and pierced sharp claws on his heart. Only he did not know why or how—he but knew there was a darkening where had been light, he but felt there was a weight where had been lightness.

And Jim? Ah, he knew, but in a half way. He was padded about with weariness, he was blinded with despair. Coming home with the smell of liquor on his breath, thinking the remote look reproach, bristling up to say, "Alright, havent I got no right to spend two bits once in a while to make me feel good? If *you* was workin under icy water all day with your head bustin from being so far underground, dancin round like a monkey to keep your footin till your can's draggin and every nerve shootin like lightning" (and, he did not say, come home to disorder and anguish) "you'd be achin for a snifter too once in a while. Aw hell, *hell*." Kicking the table leg. "Where's that Will? Runnin off with my jackknife. I'll knock the s--t out of him. And playin with all the furrin scum and niggers around. C'mon over here JimJim and sing your old pa a song. Sing for i'm a poor cowboy and I know I done wrong."

Only Mazie did not see. Still she lived on the farm in June, in early June, when a voluptuous fragrance lay over the earth. Wooden she moved about, lifting and washing and eating, and always a scarcely perceptible smile about her mouth. Mazie, a voice came shrill, you see that tub of diapers? Git to that tub of diapers. Yes, Ma. You will recite, Mazie. A hushed voice, faltering, that was she. We will have a test. And her pencil would move over the paper, separate from her guidance and her body. Sometimes a dingy sky was overhead and a

graveled playground underfoot, and her body made a
circle with other bodies. Then the schoolroom or the
walls of home would encase her again. Noise cease-
lessly rained blows upon her, the stink smothered down
into her lungs. Enveloped in the full soft dream of the
farm, she was secure. Hollow and unreal the dirty
buildings and swarming people revolved about her, flat
like a picture that her hand could smash through and
see the rolling fields and roads of home just beyond.

But terrible moments of waking would come when
the world that was about her would crash into her
dream with terrible discordant music. Fear held her
limbs there in the streets where the flats rose a tumble
of ruins, and a voice would cry: Run, run, the next
shake the houses'll fall, run, run.

And every step was pain, every look was pain, those
moments of awareness when the people streamed by
her in the streets with their hideous faces that knew her
not. Suddenly she would see before her a monster thing
with blind eyes and shaking body that gave out great
guttural sobs, a truck, she would tell herself, just a
truck, but her eyes would try to close and her feet to
run; suddenly she would see before her a woman with
her mother's face grown gaunter, holding a skeleton
baby whose stomach was pushed out like a ball, and
behind was a wall like darkness and misshapen furni-
ture. These had no reality, only the reality of night-
mares, for only there had she seen such grotesqueness
and crooked vision. And it would seem that her limbs
were crooked in sleep and a nightmare sweat was on
her, that it would be useless to resist, to cry out, because it all was a voiceless dream to be endured.

"Just see," Tracy promised, "just see. I'll make a
kick with that bastard today. Twelve foot he wants out

of us, when ten's all anything on two legs can manage."

"All right," said Jim wearily, tugging off his soggy work pants. "All right."

"And calling this a dry house," Tracy muttered. "Give me a cloudburst anytime."

"Hell, the Mississipp's a road of concrete and the ocean's a dry bed."

"How you two can beef after the day's work you put in is beyond me," old man Albright butted in, "even my tongue's laid out."

"Well, this goddam business of hangin up my work clothes in what they call a dry house and puttin em on the next morning twice as wet is just gettin under my skin."

"All right, son, wait'll you get the rheumatiz. Then you *will* have something under your skin to beef about."

"You wont see me doin any waitin," said Tracy. (I guess not, Jim thought, not till you got a woman and kids hangin around your neck.) "Look at those puckers—" pointing to his bare feet—"bigger'n on a washboard. Waterproof boots, hell. How you guys take it is beyond me."

"O.K.," said Jim, "put on the low needle and give our ears a vacation. Maybe we got something besides gettin canned up and steppin out a chippie to think about."

They dressed in silence. "Hey," Jim warned, "here comes the workingman's friend."

The contractor came in, puffed up like a balloon, with a smaller red balloon of a face wobbling on top. He spat his tobacco juice square into Jim's empty boot.

"So ten foot is all you women made today, huh? What I want to know is what the hell you do when you're on the job, suck titty?"

"Now boss," Albright said hurriedly, "we're doin the best we can. We went like a redball all day."

"You mean a standstill, dont you? Well ten's the footage all right from now on, but for two of you to manage."

"Two?" came from all their startled throats.

"Two! A miner and a mucker to a job. Miller's tried it with his monkeys and they're doin it. My crews can do as good."

"Not and stay human," Jim said.

Tracy sputtered, "It cant be done."

"Shut up—I'm the one who says what can and cant get done. Tracy and Holbrook, Marello and Albright, that's the lineup."

"But say—"

"You heard me. There's plenty good concrete men and muckers with their tongues hangin out for a job. You'll make ten or you're out."

"Not me," exploded Tracy. "I'm throwin up this sh—y job."

"O.K. by me," the contractor said, "but dont come panhandlin when you're up against it . . . Anybody else feel like the breadline?"

Nobody said anything. Jim clenched his fists. "Dirty rat," he said in his teeth, "I hope his guts wither. I hope . . ." He flung his boots and mackinaw into the locker and walked out into the dwindling light. There was a darkness in him, a heavy darkness that wound into a hardness. When the slaughterhouse workers got on before the viaduct, he pushed his way viciously out of the packed streetcar and walked into a "soft drink" parlor. "A straight," he ordered. To himself, "Alright for Tracy to talk, he doesnt have a wife and brats. But no man has any business having 'em that wants to stay a man. Having to take all that goddamn crap . . . Not that they aren't worth it though," thinking of Jimmie. "What else you got?"

The sound of the two bits clamped down on the counter brought harshly the picture of Anna counting his pay money. "Goddamn woman—what's the matter with her anyhow? Dont even have a wife that's a wife anymore—just let her say one word to me and I'll bash her head in.

He thought he saw Mazie across the street, but he was not sure. No one greeted him at the gate—the dark walls of the kitchen enclosed him like a smothering grave. Anna did not raise her head.

In the other room Bess kept squalling and squalling, and Ben was piping an out-of-tune song to quiet her. There was a sour smell of wet diapers and burned pots in the air.

"Dinner ready?" he asked heavily.

"No, not yet."

Silence. Not a word from either.

"Say, cant you stop that damn brat's squallin? A guy wants a little rest once in a while."

No answer.

"Aw, this kitchen stinks. I'm going out on the porch. And shut that brat up, she's driving me nuts, you hear?" You hear, he reiterated to himself, stumbling down the steps, you hear, you hear. Driving me nuts.

Alright for Tracy to talk, alright, he didn't have a wife and kids hangin round his neck like an anchor. Alright for him to talk, alright with nothing more important to worry about than getting canned up and stepping out a floosie.

And Tracy was young, just twenty, still wet behind the ears, and the old blinders were on him so he couldn't really see what was around and he believed the bull about freedomofopportunity and a chancetorise and ifyoureallywanttoworkyoucanalwaysfindajob and ruggedindividualism and something about pursuitofhappiness.

He didn't know, so the big sap threw it up, he threw up his job, thinking he was flinging his challenge into the teeth of life, proclaiming I'm a man, and I'm not taking crap offn anybody, I'm goin to live like a man. There's more to life than workin everything you got to live with outa you in order to keep a job, taking things no man should stand for to keep a job. So he threw it up, the big sap, not yet knowing a job was a straw and every man (having nothing to sell but his labor power) was the drowning man who had no choice but to hang onto it for notsodear life.

So he threw it up, not yet knowing a job was God, and praying wasn't enough, you had to live for It, produce for It, prostrate yourself, take anything from It, for was it not God and what came was it not by Its Divine Providence, and nothing to do but bow to It and thank It for Its mercifulness to you, a poor sinner who has nothing to sell but your labor power. So he threw it up, the big sap (not knowing), he renounced God, he became an atheist and suffered the tortures of the damned, and God Job (being full up that generation) never took him back into the fold only a few days at a time, and he learned all right what it meant to be an infidel, he learned:

the little things gone: shoeshine and tailormades, tickets to a baseball game, and a girl, a girl to love up, whiskey down your gullet, and laughter, the happy belch of a full stomach, and walking with your shoulders back, tall and proud.

He learned all right, the tortures of the damned:

feet slapping the pavement, digging humbly into carpets, squatting wide apart in front of chairs and the nojobnojob nothingdointoday buzzing in his ears; eking the coffee—and out; shuffling along the frozen streets, buddy (they made a song out of it) can you spare a dime, and the freights north east south west, getting vagged, keep movin, keep movin (the bulls dont need to tell ya, your own belly yells it out, your own idle hands) *sing a song* of hunger the weather four below holes in your pockets and nowhere to go, the flophouses, the slophouses, a bowl of misery and a last month's cruller and the crabs having a good time spreading and spreading (you didn't know hell would be this bad, did you?).

Oh he learned alright. He never even got a chance to have a wife and kids hang round his neck like an anchor and make him grovel to God Job. (And I guess it's just as well, Jim Tracy, because even among the pious who heed and prostrate themselves It's wrath is visited, for Many Are Called but Few Are Chosen, and are not the Sins of the Fathers (having nothing to sell but their labor power) Visited on the Sons, and it's no fun to see the old lady nag and worry her life away, no fun to see the younguns pulpy with charity starches drowse and chant the lesson after the teacher: we-are-the-richest-country-in-the-vorr-uld).

So (not knowing) he threw it up, the big sap, thinking, the big sap, jobs grew on trees and (believing the old bull) a man didn't hafta take crap off'n anybody, he renounced God Job—and the tortures of the damned were visited upon him in full measure, he learned alright, alright, that last hour writhing in the "piano" in the chain gang down in Florida.

And there's nothing to say, Jim Tracy, I'm sorry, Jim Tracy, sorry as hell we weren't stronger and could get to you in time and show you that kind of individual revolt was no good, kid, no good at all, you had to bide your time and take it till there were enough of you to fight it all together on the job, and bide your time, and take it till the day millions of fists clamped in yours, and you could wipe out the whole thing, the whole goddamn thing, and a human could be a human for the first time on earth.

Momma was asleep again, falling asleep right in her chair like she was always doin now, with her mouth open, and crying as if somebody was hitting her, turnin her head and crying. Ben stood looking at the little worm of water on the floor from the leaking washtub. "Ma," he called, trying not to cry, "ma." She moaned and her hands twitched at him. "Ma," he called again, louder.

She didn't wake up. Ben pushed open the kitchen door and ran out; the clothes flapping on the line slapped in his face with a crackling noise, but the wind felt good on his hot cheeks. His finger hurt awful there in the tip, like a heart was beating in it. He put it in his mouth and tried to suck the pain away.

Jimmie, stirring the ashes on the dump heap with an

old broomstick, singing, "Pudding wiv kithes, pudding wiv kithes," saw him and stood up. "Go bye?" he asked, "Ji go go go bye?"

"No," said Ben, "Momma said no." His finger throbbed and throbbed. He felt so empty inside, like when he was hungry, but the idea of food made him shudder.

"See car?" begged Jimmie, "go bye bye, see streetcar?"

"No, go on play." He pushed Jimmie down and kicked the piece of stick out of his reach.

"Go bye?" quivered Jimmie again.

"No." The yelling of it made him feel good. "No," he yelled, "no, no, no."

Near the ashes there was a tuft of fur like part of a tail of a cat. "All right, c'mon," said Ben suddenly, "we'll go bye-bye, Jimmie, far away bye."

"Go go go," sang Jimmie, collecting his broken bits of wood, "go go go."

Up at the corner big men were standing around laughing. Through their legs Ben could see a dog, a dog like Shep. One held him by the collar, and another was sticking nails all over a piece of meat. "The funniest sight you ever did see," he chortled, "the way a dawg tries to get at the meat."

"Shep," called Ben, "here, Shep, here, Shep."

The man in front turned around. "That aint your dog. Scram!"

"Maybe it is," faltered Ben. "Shep, here, Shep."

"Say, I said beat it, you and your shadow. Go on home and get some titty."

"No, I wanna see."

"Scram now." The man pushed his shoe into Ben's back and gave him a shove. "Go on."

Ben ran. But Jimmie tugged back. "See streetcar," he wept, "see car." In vain Ben pulled and pulled, finally Jimmie gave. Then tears came, and in the middle of the tears an anger lashing. Ben picked up a rock and smashed it against the telephone pole, he pounded, pounded the pavement. Frightened, Jimmie began to cry too.

"Aw hush up," Ben savagely commanded. "Hush up, nuffin to cry about, nuffin. You heard me," pushing him down. "You heard me." Then: "I'm sorry, Jimmie, please dont cry JimJim, we'll go see a streetcar, we'll go see a car, we'll go see a car. Please dont cry." Seeing Mazie come down the street, slowly, dreamily, a paper clutched in her hand: "See, Mazie'll take us bye-bye." But she walked past.

Bess was wailing. "Ma," said Mazie, shaking her, "wake up, baby's cryin, she wants to nurse."

With her mouth open (so far in some sharp livid place), Anna slept on, drawing deep hoarse breaths.

"*Ma,*" yelled Mazie again, "baby's cryin, wake up, wake up."

Anna's body became rigid, then convulsed. She sprang out of her chair with a cry, trembling. "What?" she asked in a voice not her own, "What? . . . Oh." The kitchen, the half-done wash, a glimmering face like Mazie's. She pushed her hand hard over her brow. "Must've been asleep. Now . . . what did you say, Mazie?"

"Bess's cryin, Momma."

"Yes, Bess's cryin." It seemed Mazie's face dipped and swayed like a sea. All that heaviness . . . to batter through. "Better bring her in here." Sinking again. Then with a start: "My land, you home already? I musta been asleep a long time. And dinner to get, and still clothes to get out on the line. I'm gettin up right now" (but she sank right back in the chair). "Will home yet?"

"No'm." An absent smile. "He said he was gonna play ball."

The room would not come clear. Such a burning somewhere, such a swimming and a haze. Bess's cry lost and struggling somewhere. "Hush, baby," she said automatically, pulling out her breast. "Hush now." Calling, "Mazie."

With such an effort she managed to find the thought and push it out steady. "Better go get a pail of lard down at the store and tell him to put it on the bill. Say please. Best bring a diaper first."

The room swimming, swimming, or was it she? Bess did not seem to be at her breast at all. Soaked, soaked through to the bone, she thought, but her fingers felt no wet. She tried to rise. A great wave of giddiness and illness rose and waited to engulf her; she sank back down. "Them clothes, I guess. Leavin me tired enough not to move for a thousand years."

Cleanly, suddenly, she arose and stumbled to the table. There, it was alright now. She lay Bess down and took off her wet diaper and put on another. The paper Mazie had laid there danced before her eyes, so she could not read it. A long while before she made out the words.

It would have struck her like a blow on the naked heart once, this failure report from school, but now she folded it carefully and put it into her pocket. "You bring another one and I'll beat you to a pulp," she said to the empty room. To Bess, "Dont you know learnin's the only hope a body's got in this world?" And her lips curved in a smile, remembering the remote dream look in Mazie's eyes as if she were not there at all. "I aim to see any kids we have happy, Jim, not like we were brought up. Happy and with learnin." Her hand lifted to caress his cheek.

Shuddering, she clutched the table edge. "Hold on, Anna old girl," she said to herself. "Hold on." Gettin a little teched in the head from the heat, I guess, she explained carefully. The wave of pain gathered her up, engulfed her, so that she swayed. Where . . . was . . . that . . . chair? God she *was* sick. Sick enough to die. The quivering in her back and the pounding in her head. "Will," she called faintly, "Mazie." Oughta know they wouldn't be around when you want them, and it was you sent Mazie off to the store, she reminded herself scornfully.

A terrible sobbing anguished her ears. Stop it, Anna, she begged, stop it, dont be such a baby. But it was only Bess crying. Only . . . Bess. What's the matter with you anyhow? There, it was going to happen again, the dizziness and pain. She sank down to the chair, down, down as far as she could go, and the pounding of her heart filled the world.

After a while she lifted her head. "I'd better jest set here a while yet," she said out loud, "but not for long. I cant let Jim find me like this."

Ben's face was so red and funny. Could he have been listening or watching there at the kitchen door? "It's about time," she managed to say as loud as she could. "I thought I told you not to go away."

"Didnt, didnt, dont care." He turned around to go.

"C'mon back here, you . . . Oh." It was a cry of anguish. Trying to rise, the waters of pain had closed over her head again, and a terrible something, hovering, had sunk its claws in her back.

"Oh, Momma," begged Ben, running back, "dont be sick."

"No, Ben, Momma's not sick." Faintly, "But can you hold Bess and not —(it was better now)— drop her? Just put her down . . . in the basket."

Jimmie here too. But best dont get up. Sit here and let your strength gather up. (The main thing, not to wander off, not to let the fever bear her away.) "Ben, you and Jimmie want to help Momma make dinner now? You bring me the pan over there and a knife, first, Ben, and you and Jimmie take the potatoes out of the sack, and bring them to me till I tell you to stop. Thats right. Thats right."

Clutching a pail of lard, dreaming a sweet dream of twilight on the farm and darkening over a fragrant world, her face not shadowed by the buildings above, her nostrils not twitching with the stink in the air, her eyes not bewildered by the seething of people about her, dreaming the sweet dream unutterable, a hard body crashed into her and a voice thundered: "Whynt you look where you're going, stinking little bitch," and she was pushed in the stomach, punched down sprawling, a drunken breath in her nostrils. (Fear remembered such a breath. It seemed a mass pressed itself into her face, wet earth, or something she did not remember. In a minute she would be lifted and carried through a blackness of terror.) A wet was on her cheek, not blood, but a blob of spit she had fallen into. Feeling it, shuddering awoke her veins. She struggled to get up. Harsh, the pavement grated against her. It was real then. She moved her hand over the walk. Yes, it was real.

A streetcar plunged shrieking down the street, scraping over a naked nerve. Set, intent faces passed by. Terrible faces, masked in weariness and hate and lust, faces that knew her not, that saw her not.

The long street stretched infinite, a space that could never be finished traveling over, distorted buildings blocking each side. There was no sky, only a slab of one, draining color, vanishing into darkness.

She put her arm around the lamppost. Its solidity was fearful to her. As for the first time she saw the street and people, and it entered into her like death. A woman was sitting in the basement window in front of her, a great black around her eyes, teeth bared in a terrible smile. A man in a soldier's uniform, seeing her, staggered down the steps. The window blind went down. Real then, real.

The trembling, vibrating sound in the lamppost like a wild imprisoned heart. She sprang away. A shriek from behind. Slowly, slowly, with such laboriousness she turned her head. A bum was hurtling out of an eating joint, hitting the sidewalk, and the man coming after, roaring: "Dont ever try that again, you rat, or you wont have a face left or a belly." He gave him a kick, the body stopped sliding, he kicked him again and again. Faces distorted into laughter, and from the street around a fearful sound of hoarse joy went up into the sky.

Mazie ran. She fell. Here near the top of the street, she could see the shattered sun die in a sky of bruises over the decayed line of houses and buildings. Way down, like a hog, a great hulk of building wallowed. A-R-M-O-U-R-S gray letters shrieked. Armours, said Mazie over and over: Armoursarmoursarmours. Beautiful, suspended, the farm, softened by twilight floated an instant before her eyes. A new bulk, "C'mon, hand it over," shattered it forever. It passed her, and Mazie could see it was two people, and the man was twisting the woman's arm. Armoursarmours. Every step was pain, every look was pain. The spit felt on her face again and the terrible face of the soldier as he ran down the stairs thickened her in horror that over it held the shadow of something mushy, opening in the middle, pressed hard against her cheeks.

Only a block to home. She began to run, running, trying to run away from the stink, away from the street, back, back, to something that had never been. Mr. Kryckszi held her arm. He was all stink, all stink, he helped kill cows, cows like Brindle, and Annamae said he washed blood off himself. "Come, little one," he said in his funny English (he was a furriner), "do not hasten so. Life will catch up with you soon enough. Let us walk together."

There was a man with him, something wrong with his shoulders, so he hunched over, misshapen. They walked along in silence. But their shoes made an awful sound. Long shadows lay over the street; the wind—flinging the arc lamp—twitched them as if they were alive. Mazie was glad for Kryckszi's hand, and she held it tight, tight.

There was no light in the house, as if nobody was home. Her father sat on the steps, weariness riding his shoulders like despair. Kryckszi called through the windy dark: "You not try to get on at the yards any more, Holbrook?"

"Naw."

"Today they hire."

"Damn shame you aint a nigger," the other man interrupted. "If you was you could get on in a minute."

"Today they hire," Kryckszi said again. "They think you are scissors bill maybe they take you too—that is why they taking blacks—they think they scab if there is strike—*have* to scab, how else they get job?"

Mazie went up to her father. He did not even look at her. Flat, inflectionless, he spoke: "Git in there and help your ma git dinner on the table. You might tell her Bess aint the only one in the house that wants to eat."

There was something she wanted to say, but she could not remember it. "Go on," her father harshly ordered, "get in there."

The light was not on. In the dirty light of dusk her mother sat motionless, her eyes large and feverish, the baby at her breast asleep. The lifeless hair hung in two black braids, framing her like a coffin, and above a spiral of fire foamed, reflected from the open damper. "Momma," said Mazie for no reason and went up and kissed her. The cheek was burning to her lips.

Armoursarmours, her lips said soundlessly, and she slipped to her knees and buried her face in her mother's lap.

Her mother did not move. Mazie clutched her closer. The limbs began to tremble. "Yes," her mother spoke, "I never was much of a hand for tonics, but when it gets you like this, Else . . ."

Mazie pushed herself away. The nightmare feeling came back. But the table felt solid against her back (the pavement grated her hand, harsh). In the darkness she brought out the dishes and put them on the table. She opened the oven and fed it wood.

Up above her mother's head the swirl of color foamed larger and larger. Suddenly it brought a nausea of fear (the jelly mass pushing against her face, the breath stinking, the shuddering laugh). She ran for the lamp and turned it up and stood there in the sudden light, trembling. There, it was gone now.

"What?" a hoarse, startled, fear-stricken sound from Anna. "What?" then realizing: "Oh . . . the light. Musta startled me. Where you been so long, Missy? Better get the table set and the bread cut. Poppa'll be home any minute now."

"Poppa *is* home," stubbornly, "he is. The table's set and Poppa *is* home."

"Yes. Poppa is home. I'll put Bess to bed and we'll eat." Falling on her knees in front of the oven as if she were praying, "I guess nothin burned. You can take the bean pot out and turn the potatoes into a dish. And cal your dad. . . . Why, baby," sensing her vibrating body, "dont tremble so. You didnt think I was goin to hit you, did you? What made you think that? I wasnt going to touch you."

And Will coming in—Will? This stranger with the dirt on his cheek like a bruise and the sullen gray eyes? "Oh boy, are you goin to get it for flunkin. Oh boy, you'll be so raw you wont be able to sit down for a millyun years," without zest. "Oh boy, wait till Ma tells Pa . . . Who you sayin shut up to," pushing her against the wall.

Perhaps it frightens you as you walk by, the travail of the trees against the dark crouched house, the weak tipsy light in the window, the man sitting on the porch, menacing weariness riding his flesh like despair. And you hurry along, afraid of the black forsaken streets, the crooked streets, and look no more. But there are those who have looked too much through such windows, seeing the pain on everything, the darkening pain twisting and writhing over the faces, over and about the lamp like a wind to blow the flame out.

The pain, the darkening pain on everything. And it seemed to Mazie that her limbs were crooked in sleep and a nightmare sweat were on her, for only there had she seen such grotesqueness and crooked vision. And Anna struggling to keep her head clear and far above. They sat there at the meal in silence, only Jimmie chattering away, Will choking his food down as if he never expected to eat again. Once Jim pushed his plate away and said clearly, distinctly (against the darkening pain) "Any time I want sewage to eat I can get it on the job," but it seemed no one heard, and hastily he pulled the plate back and shoved the food down.

The stink of burning bacon grease in the air. Reaching for the frying pan, for the burning handle, with a bellow Jim dropped it, and with one kick sent it flying to the door, with another kick out into the yard, then turned (is the burn in his hand? it seems to be burning far inside, a scorch that will not let him be), facing Anna, facing Will, who laughs louder and louder, facing Mazie, who stares (useless to resist, to cry out, because it all is a voiceless dream to be endured), and Ben, who pales. "So ya think it's funny, do ya?" not knowing it is a chair he holds in his hand and is crashing toward Will, ducking under the table. She wrenches herself free from the battering pain. "You crazy?" slapping his face savagely. "You gone crazy? You coulda crippled Will. Set down everybody and finish eatin. It's all right, kids, everything's all right. If you hold out your hand—I'll smear oleo on so it wont blister. Jim? Set down, you hear! Please?" And he sinks down, the madness ebbing. Fearful what it leaves behind, the shame.

And perhaps it all would have been all right, that night anyhow, but after supper Ben (so wanting love) buried his face in his father's big shoulders and proffered his finger for sympathy. Shocked, righteous, Jim told Anna (not seeing how she clutched the sink rim between dishes), "Dont you pay no attention to these kids? You do something right away about Ben's finger. It's swoll up like a tire. What do you mean lettin it go like that? Better soak it, draw the splinter out."

She put on the water to heat, poured Purex into a glass, but after she'd mixed the boiling water (pain's hand in hers, and all else fled) she forgot that hot was hot and plunged Ben's finger in. And still held it against Ben's scream and writhing till Jim knocked the glass out from under. "You crazy" was all he could say. "You crazy . . . This madhouse. I'm clearin out."

She managed through the nursing, she managed through the loving till Ben was comforted and through the sharp commands till the others quieted, and then she fainted. Now she should have called WillMazieBen, for they were fled into a terror which nothing could reach. When Mis' Kryckszi came, gleaning only from Ben's skirt tugging and incoherent mommamomma, something terrible had happened, Anna lay peacefully as if she were drowned, in a pool of water, and Will was pouring over more, and Mazie was shaking her and begging, "Wake up, wake up."

Vinegar on her nostrils and wrist-chafing, and Anna cleft back from the tranquility and the quietness. Lucky the pain that bore her into its own world, so she could not see her children's faces; lucky the numbness of sleep that came after.

Mis' Kryckszi said nothing, carrying sleeping Jimmie from the front-room floor onto his cot, mopping up the floor, bathing the children's hot faces, but after it all was done, she took Ben on her lap and sang to them, not lullabies, but songs of her own country in which her fierce anger flashed.

Lurching down the streets, his face lifted to the

stars, singing out his great crude singing, feeling the wind like a flame against him, singing against the night and the wind—so that the little Negro boy, Jeff, on the corner, waking smiled and hummed softly to himself, and heard a humming in his head like a thousand telegraph wires, a thousand messages of sound that would blend into music—singing his wide crude singing (I hear America singing, the varied carols I hear) so that the vast night throbbed about him, Jim came home.

Mazie, her head under the bedclothes, trying to stifle the fear and horror that retched within her, heard the singing; heard the door slammed shut, the thudding steps, the toilet flushed, the drunken talk her father had with himself that the rising wind enclosed, swept away.

No use to tell him, not a bit of use, stiffly repeated itself and marched round and round her head. No use, no use.

What was happening? It seemed the darkness bristled with blood, with horror. The shaking of the bed as if someone were sobbing in it, the wind burrowing through the leaves filling the night with a shaken sound. And the words, the words leaping.

"Dont, Jim, dont. It hurts too much. No, Jim, no."

"Cant screw my own wife. Expect me to go to a whore? Hold still."

The merciful blood pounding in Mazie's ears, battering away the sounds. Oh Will. Crawl up close, put your arms around, you'll feel better. Soundless: O Will, Will. He hears too? The hoarse breathing—the moan?

As if in sleep (pretend sleep?): "Get away from me, ya damn girl."

Ben in his sleep, sucking in his breath sharp and wounded, Jimmie in his sleep, blowing out a soft bubble of sound.

"Will, somethin's happened to Momma. *Will*." Al-

right, act asleep. I'll pretend asleep too. Lay down
heart, go to sleep. Poppa, quit shakin me. No Poppa
here—you shakin yourself. Alright, I'll get up.

Oh, Ma, Ma. The blood on the kitchen floor, the
two lifeless braids of hair framing her face like a
corpse, the wall like darkness behind. Be away, Mazie,
be away. "Poppa, come in the kitchen, Momma went
dead again, Poppa, come on." The drunken breath.
(Fear remembered such a breath.) So cruel the way he
pushes her away, uncomprehending. "Lemme sleep."

"Oh Poppa," crying now, "Momma's dead again.
Please, Poppa, please come."

Running back to the kitchen (so ugly: Momma, all
the hair, the blood) running back with water, calling
"Poppa" again till he somehow comprehends and
comes. How clumsily he lifts Anna and carries her to
the bed and brings the lamp. And remembering something of what Bess Ellis had done after the baby was
born; with tremor hands he kneads the flesh above her
womb till the blood stops pouring, and stillness comes.

What does Bess have to wake up again and cry for?
Poppa gone, and I dont know what to do. Dont cry,
baby, dont cry. The lamp dancin, dancin. Whats the
matter with you, lamp, what you see so funny you
hafta dance about? Daddy singing when he comes
home like the world is all strong and singin; and the
wind—hear the wind in the trees, cryin for people that
cant cry no more, crying for people that want to cry
and cant. Oh Momma, dont talk like that. ("So sweet
Jim, a little oyster, a little pearl, a growin . . . No,
Bess . . . not bad, only I wish the bearin-down pains
would start. Oh." Such a shriek. "Elma, be careful
. . . All Elma's fingers gone, Ma, just a stump a
bleedin left. I didnt know so much blood was in a

body. And the damn forelady yelling, go on back to work . . .") No, Momma, no, Bess, dont cry. I'll hold ya and love ya, Bess, I'll tell ya a story, see, I'll diaper you and I'll tell you a story, onct upon a time the night was quiet, and the river, a cool river, Bess, was goin along, goin along, talkin to itself so happy, and it said maybe Bess would like to come and Mazie too and it dont go by no cities, Bess. Stop cryin, Bess, even baby's cryin (so ugly the naked thigh, the coarse hair, all the blood), please, somebody, oh Momma, stop talkin.

And the lamp in the wind from the open windows and the twitching shadows, the writhing of the trees, the waiting and words in fever and delirium.

He is back. He sits there immolated, a frieze, holding Anna's hand, and Mazie, so cold, clutches Bess, frightened of going back into the night of the bedroom, back with Will *(get away from me, ya damn girl)*. And they wait till the doctor comes.

"Miscarriage. You didn't know she was pregnant—again?" And Mazie runs *(on the kitchen floor the blood)* runs, runs outside.

"How old's the baby?" (Damn fools, they ought to sterilize the whole lot of them after the second kid.)

"Four months, mm. You remember how long your wife's been feeling sick?" Of course not. These animals never notice but when they're hungry or want a drink or a woman.

"Hmmmm. Yes." She took the ergot down quietly, but moaned at the hypo. "So you had intercourse before, it wasn't only the fall." (Pigsty, the way these people live.) "And she's been nursing all along? We'll have a look at the baby." (Rickets, thrush, dehydrated; don't blame it trying to die.) "Viosterol is what it needs—and a dextri-maltose formula.

"Your wife's a sick woman. Needs all the rest she can get, fresh fruits, vegetables, and liver. And medical attention. So does the baby. Unless you can afford a private doctor, see she gets to the clinic for a curettage—that's a cleaning out. And the baby's to be weaned right away—I'm writing it all down here—wait a minute, there's a change. Karo syrup and canned milk for the formula; try to get some cod-liver oil—the baby really needs it—or at least all the sun it can stand with most of its skin exposed."

Running, so much ugliness, the coarse hair, the night bristling, the blood and the drunken breath and the blob of spit, something soft, mushy, pressed against her face, never the farm, dont cry, even baby's cryin, get away from me ya damn girl, the faint gray vapor of river, run, run, but it scares you so, the shadows the lamp throws in the wind.

The cold, the world was so cold, she was wearing her slip and barefoot, and seeing the lamppost, she clutched it, trying to press the trembling vibrating thing inside her, back into where she had first heard it. And her eyes lifted in horror . . . lifted in horror that wavered and broke.

Globed and golden in the green light of early dawn, the street lamps stretched far and far. Beside them crouched the solid rows of buildings, little weak lights in their windows, and down in the valley, solid and quiet, the great mass of packing house and stockyard. The viaduct was laced in fairy lines, and against the sky four great smoke stacks reared, so strong, so beautiful in the glowing light with the fading smoke rising out of their throats, she could not help it, her arms reached out as if to touch and embrace them. A shudder went over her body, a shudder of quietness, and then tears, through which the beautiful street shimmered and was diamonded, the street lamps rayed and haloed.

He lifted her and carried her toward home, her father. "Were you scared, were you scared? Momma's sick, awful sick, Bigeyes. Awfully sick, and the doctor says she needs everything she cant get, tells me everything she needs, but not how to get it (cry from a million swollen throats), everything she needs but not how to get it. You're so cold, kiddie. Why do you want to go back to the top of the street for? Kiss Poppa and we'll go home and I'll make a farm and warm you, a nice fire, and you can fall asleep on daddy's lap . . .

"And Bess' pretty sick, me not noticing, blind as a bat. And medicine, he says. Everything, but not how to get it. Stop shivering, baby. We'll make a big fire and warm you up."

No, he could speak no more. Watching the flame catch and sputter and die and leap up again. Covering up Anna and the baby. No, he could speak no more. And as he sat there in the kitchen with Mazie against his heart, and dawn beat up like a drum, the things in his mind so vast and formless, so terrible and bitter, cannot be spoken, will never be spoken—till the day that hands will find a way to speak this: hands.

SIX

Two days she lay there quietly, in a merciful numbness that was half sleep, half coma, emerging out of it once to say: I'll be getting up now, Else, but making no move to, just lying there, tracing with her eyes the stains on the ceiling, sinking back into the twilight dimness again. Once Bess's fretful piping pierced into her dream, and with trembling fingers she pulled her breast out, trying to rise to the baby. Ben, playing by the bed, saw and ran for Else. She came in time to hold the struggling woman down, saying over and over, Lie still, honey, go on back to sleep, lie still, till Anna gave way and turned on her pillow and closed her eyes. After that, Bess was kept daytimes out in the yard, beyond hearing.

Wild with the exultance of the first vacation days, Mazie and Will were off somewhere. Quarrels flared in the kitchen when they came in on their forays for food. "I declare, I dont know whats the matter with you," Else would say, "carryin on so with your ma sick in bed in the next room, needin every bit of rest she can get. Aint you shamed pickin on your sister, Will? And you, Mazie, you oughta be home lookin after Jimmie and Ben, you're the little mother now. Come back here, where you runnin off to again, *come back,*" the last yelled to figures vanishing with their loot of bread and shortening. And then the house would stand empty and quiet again, save for Else's padding about and the shuffle of Ben's pieces of cloth as he arranged and rearranged them in pattern play on the floor by Anna's bed.

And at five when Else left, the stillness deepened and darkened, the late-afternoon sunlight filling the rooms with a haze golden and tranquil, gilding the face of Will as he crept in to look at his mother, flickering over Mazie taking up Bess to see if she needed changing, haloing little Jimmie's head as he crept in, weary and dirty. And in the stillness, Will and Mazie would lift down the heavy pots and Mazie fill the plates and together bring them out on the back stoop, where they sat, Mazie and Will and Ben and Jimmie, watching the sun fire up the sky, burst and fade, while they ate their supper.

And at seven Mrs. Kryckszi would come, quieting Bess till her bottle was ready, crooning softly while she fed her, washing up Ben and Jim for the night; and last with the last darkening—Jim—to eat his solitary meal in silence, to tend Ben's finger and round up the older children, and sit there in the soft dark, whittling, trying to figure a way out on the money, prodding himself to stay awake, fumbling through another feeding for Bess so he could go to bed at last; and the house stand there in its curious empty stillness till dawn, and the same day begin again.

The third day, Jim's Sunday off, began a tossing. Whenever Jim came in she would be lying with her head turned toward the window, asleep, he would have thought, except for the staring eyes and the hand that quivered at her throat. Go back to sleep, he would say, best sleep again, but she never answered, answered or looked at him or questioned why it was that she was lying there, or what had happened. Once he heard her whimper: O my breasts, they sting so, they're so full, but hearing him approach, she turned her face sharply away, asking in a voice not hers: "Is Bess eating all right?" But before he could answer, her eyes were closed and she was lying in a semblance of sleep he did not disturb.

Helped up, supported by Else, still in the seeming quietude, she went to the clinic, clutching the doctor's slip of paper Jim had put in her purse to give. Else, by her side, could not get a word out of her. But sitting in the clinic, waiting in the smell of corroding and the faces of pain, she lifted Bess out of Else's lap, shielded her close and rasped out fiercely: "We shouldn'ta brought baby here, we shouldn'ta brought her." And all the way home—against the frowsy houses and streets of filth the streetcar jolted past—she hugged the squalling child to her.

Home, clutching the pillow to her inflamed breasts as if she still held Bess, she sank into an exhausted sleep into which the distorted faces of pain at the clinic marched round and round in endlessly dragging regiments of themselves.

In the kitchen Jim was saying to Mrs. Kryckszi, stitching at a canvas: "One way to swell up the paycheck anyhow. No more soakin me for the waterproofs and boots every week. But do you think I'm gettin back one cent of all I been payin in? Not one cent. They said did I think they was in the equipment rentin business?" Then he saw Anna in the doorway.

"Anna! You aint supposed to be up. Was you needin somethin?"

". . . The house . . . It needs cleanin."

"And you're in fine shape to do it. Get back to bed."

In a mesmerized voice. "Dirt, the poster said. Dirt . . ."

"Ferget it. You ain't supposed to be up."

". . . Breeds Disease. Disease . . ."

"Outa her mind," he explained to Mrs. Kryckszi. "C'mon now." At her side, but hesitant to touch her. "Back to bed. You lost a lot of blood."

"Germs spread . . ." She recoiled from his touch, said in notice: "Why, Mis' Kryckszi!" cordially, naturally; relapsed again into the haunted voice. "Your children . . . Con-ta-gion . . . O, the posters."

"You been awful sick. Come along now."

"The house . . ." Wringing her hands. "At the clinic, they scare you. And all the poor sick people setting . . ."

"Don't worry your head. Get under them covers."

". . . All the poor sick people waitin. So many ways of being sick. And we shouldnta brought baby there, we shouldnta took her."

"I said dont worry your head. Cover up good now."

Her hands clenched. She looked at him sharply, bitterly; mutely turned her head away.

"You want anything, just holler. Sleep now, you hear?" He did not leave her till it seemed she slept.

Back in the kitchen, miserable, he watched the needle glitter in and out of the stiff poncho. He yearned to ask Mrs. Kryckszi about Anna but could form neither words nor thoughts.

"It fit now, I think," she said at last, folding up the canvas and handing it to him. "Try on." Then, with a nod toward the bedroom: "She begin to get better now. She begin to feel things again. You be careful with her now."

She lay there a long while after she awoke, trying to make out what time it could be. If there had been rain, it was over now. Dust motes were gleaming in the shaft of light that slanted in through the window. The house seemed empty. "Else, Ben," she called softly. No one answered. Slowly she pulled herself up and edging along the wall, pushed open the door into the front room. It lay in shadow, and out of an old enlarged photo, a very young Anna with a baby Will in her arms smiled down upon her. Her face contorted. Quickly she closed the door.

She had not wanted to go through the bathroom but there was no other way now. High up in a dirty brown corner, a cobweb spangled. Unsteadily she picked up the plunger and swept it down. One fly, still alive, moved an iridescent wing and buzzed. The kitchen stood blank and empty in glaring afternoon sun. It was a long while before she could make out the potato peels turning black on the garbage in the sink, the dirty dishes, the souring bottle of milk about which flies droned. Flies, the poster said, Spread Germs. Germs Breed Disease. Cleaving to the table for support, disregarding the flame of agony in her engorged breasts, she swatted feverishly. The flies lifted and evaded. Disease . . . Your children . . . Protect . . . The soap was gone, the water spluttered malevolently at her. She rinsed the dishes, scooped the garbage up into a pot, and went out into the yard. It was deserted but for Bess sleeping in her basket, covered with an old curtain for netting.

Someone had forgotten to put the cover on the garbage pail, and below the solid droning mass of flies, gray things slithered and struggled. The stench steamed up and hit her in the nostrils. Gasping for breath, she threw the garbage in, pot and all, and jammed the cover on, then stumbled over to the stoop and sat down. The vomit kept rising and rising, but none came. Didnt know I was so delicate, she whispered. Whew. Whew. And jest garbage smell mixed in with a little packinhouse.

All the time it kept nagging, the pot still there, the pot she could not replace. Scarcely realizing that she was doing so, she pulled herself erect by the screen-door handle and, half falling, got back to the pail. The flies sprang to her face as before and the stench retched up, but she stood there stubbornly, with head averted and nostrils stiffened, clutching for the slippery surface of the pot.

This time she barely managed to reach the stoop. Her limbs were trembling, her bones seemed water, her heavy breasts burned, burned. All she could do was sit there, her head against the screen door, her eyes closed, waiting for the trembling and faintness to cease. Slowly, slowly, her fingers loosened, and the pot slipped from her hand to the ground.

It was very quiet. The sun lay warm on her shoulders, and far off through the muted voices of the street a peddler was calling, his voice reminding of an old song. Softly she began to sing. Now a train puffed by, and the long wail dissolved in distance. The wind just lifted against her cheek. Ben came from nowhere and nuzzled against her. Momma, he said. She held him warm into her singing.

"Momma." She opened her eyes and saw his eye-lashes fluttering over the patches of rash on his cheek; the dirty sore on his unbandaged finger; the stubble ground, the harsh curtain that made the netting on Bess's basket,—and beyond, far beyond, white foam of bridal wreath on the sea blue sky.

White bridal wreath. When she was a girl . . . O when she was a girl . . . The life she had dreamed and the life that had come to be . . . The scabby sore on Ben's finger scratched against her arm, the vagrant wind retched the garbage smell. She closed her eyes again, but this time when she opened them, her fists were clenched, and Ben she had held so close to her was pushed away. Whether or not she said it aloud, a cry throbbed in the air: *No. No.*

She had wrapped a rag around the broom and swept down the walls, and swept the floors, and scrubbed the toilet bowl, and put the diapers to soak, and was filling a tub with water preparatory to scrubbing the floor, when Mrs. Kryckszi came in with Mazie and Jimmie.

"You been cleanin, Anna?" Mrs. Kryckszi asked, incredulous. "You go to bed." Then, seeing the stubborn face flaring white behind its fury, in harder tones: "What the matter? You want to stay sick? Cleanin going to wait for you, it not going noplace. You go lay down."

"I *been* layin down. As for you, Missy," seeing Mazie, "where have *you* been? Git in here. There's work for you to do."

"Annamae's waitin." Defiantly: "I gotta play." Then with sullen averted face: "Poppa says you'll get . . . that way again if you don't stay in bed."

"Poppa says! . . . Annamae's got a long wait, sister. Git in now and git started. You hear me? Now if you'll excuse us, Mis' Kryckszi, and I want to thank you for all you been doing, I'll get back to my work."

ing hoarsely. "Who's to care about 'em if we dont? Who?"

Fighting off his attempt to enfold her, to quiet; his broken: "Anna, dont, please dont."

"Who? Answer me . . . Oh Jim," giving in, collapsing into his reaching embrace, "the children." Over and over, broken: "the children. What's going to happen with them? How we going to look out for them? O Jim, the children. Seems like we cant do nothing for them in this damn world."

O Will, hoe in hand chopping viciously the air, running down the block away from his father's stricken face, his mother's convulsed words; o Ben, clutching first his mother's legs and then his father's legs, trying vainly to still them, curling up now close to Mazie, heaving his asthma breaths; o Mazie, stopping up her ears so as not to hear, yelling out a song to Jimmie and to clinging Ben so they will not hear—it is alright, it is over now.

It is over. There is reconciliation in the house where your mother lies weeping; not hearing the *I'll spade up the garden and tomorrow, payday, we'll get seeds. We'll work things out, you'll see, dont take on so;* hearing only the attempt at comfort. And now your father lies beside her, stroking and kissing her hair, silently making old vows again, vows that life will never let him keep.

SEVEN

Always while Jim worked (—*down underground the dripping water diamonds his hair, trickles down his neck, makes a gay sound on his canvas poncho: no mackinaw and boots, but it means a buck more a week dont it, it means stuff for the baby, dont it?*—) heavy and sore in his breast would lay the torment of the questions Anna had asked, and such a sad baffled flame of tenderness flicker above.

Work through, with a heart that ran far ahead of his feet, he would hurry, hurry home, a nameless fear on him, and his hello be almost a sob of joy as he flung open the door and saw that all seemed as it had been.

A gaunt Anna who could not understand this body of hers that tired so quickly and quivered like a naked nerve; this stranger self. One minute her old competence and strength; the next: addled, nervous, brutal, lost. Not managing, having to give under, to let things go. Any effort wearing her out; everything an effort.

Seeing her so, with the look of exhaustion on him, Jim would ask: "Is there anything I can do to help?"

Sometimes she did not answer at all, sometimes say: "You look right tired, why don't you go ahead and set." But once she blazed: "If you cant see what *needs* doin, just dont trouble to ask, you hear, just dont trouble to ask." And another time, in the most chilling of voices: "Why dont you go set like you always do; done." Adding: "'Cept that one wintertime on the farm I was carryin Bess. And that didn't last long."

Now, in her slow mending, she began to ask him to chase the kids down, or to chide, or distract them. "They're runnen me crazy. I declare I dont know what's got into 'em, seems like the devil hisself."

Ben whining or wanting to be babied, afraid to let his mother out of sight, always underfoot with questions. Go out, she would force him, go out and play. Go on. But he huddled close to the kitchen door, his only playmate Jeff and sometimes Jimmie. Jimmie at an age where he was always having to be watched, likely to get into any manner of mischief. Will defiant; Mazie contrary—too exhausting to force their help (and the feeling: they're kids, let them play and feel good while they can).

Troubled, she saw them running, shrilling out laughter, playing their frantic games wildly, disappearing to come back hours later; flushed, hostile, excited, secretive. A lust for sensation, for the new was on them, a lust for the streets, for looking into store windows; for moving over the dump, the stretches of weed and alley. They clamored for pennies she did not have for licorice, shoestrings, blackjacks, jawbreakers, Juicy Fruit gum—litany of wonders endless at the corner store; on Saturdays, for nickels to go to the movie show. No, she had to say over and over, we dont have it, no—but sometimes if she had it set aside for another purpose, she gave them what they asked.

She began to neglect the already neglected house to go out and weed and work in the garden. The washtubs and wringer sat out in the yard now, beside Bess's basket. She would have liked to range the stove alongside too, even cook over an open fire. Inside suffocated her (outside too when there was packing-house stench) but a need was in her to be out under a boundless sky, in unconfined air, not between walls, under the roof of a house.

The cumulating vision of hostile, overwhelming forces surrounding which had come to Anna that week of the clinic, never left her. But she was not strong enough to contend with it yet. Only sporadically could she try to order, do something about their lives. And a separation, a distance—something broken and new and tremulous—had been born in her, lying by herself those long unaccustomed hours free of task.

One dusktime, when Jim got home, she and Mazie were still wringing and hanging clothes. "Get in and see to supper, Mazie, while I finish up out here," Anna said, seeing him. Cheerfully: "I got my first launderin job today."

"I see that." Sinking down heavily onto the stoop as the light drained. Bitterly: "You aint well enough to keep us 'uns clean, or get your other work done like you used to, let alone do for other folks."

"What's well enough or other work got to do with—have to?" she asked, and went on hanging up what was left in the basket; took down blouses, shirts, dresses from another line.

"I said you aint well enough for what you got to do for us 'uns now. We never lived in such a mess."

"It's a dollar every time." . . . Dreamily: "That looks nice across the river, dont it? The mist comin up like way away soft laundry blowin on a line. White."

"You fixin to get sick on me again? . . . Ferget that launderin, Anna. We'll get by. We ain't starved yet."

She looked at him with an expression that, in the uncertain light, he thought might be anger or bitterness, but her voice came humble: "I'm helpin, Jim." She came over, her arms heaped; sagged beside him. "Feels good to sit, dont it? You look mighty weary." Carefully she smoothed and rolled the garments, arranged them in the basket.

"That's pretty how you do that," said Ben, rising from the shadows. "Are you making it a sunflower? Can I try tree and branches?"

"You touch that wash with your dirty hands, and you'll never touch another thing. How long since you washed up?"

"Bess was laughin and laughin today, Poppa," Ben reported. "Lookin cross-eyed at her hands, so *we* got laughin. When I say, 'Bessie, Bess, Bonny Bess,' she turns and looks for me, dont she, Momma? Do you have a penny for Will? Your hair's still wet, Poppa."

"How's yourself, old tricks?" drawing Ben close. "I got a penny for *you*, all right."

"Jim, a man came by today and for a quarter a week if we start now, a kid gets three hundred dollars when he's sixteen. For a sure edjication."

Jim jabbed at Ben's arm, shadow-punched at his face. "Dont you know how to duck yet?"

Holding his father's hand to stay it: "Guess what, Poppa? We blewed soap bubbles today with green onions. Momma showed us how. All shiny. Mine was the biggest, then Mazie's. Where do bubbles go with your breath when they bust, Poppa? Where's gone? What does nothing look like, Poppa?"

"I want it for Will, then he can help the others. Finish high school sure. A good job, Jim."

"You think I dont want it? Even to be sneakin time-keepers and office people that treats you like dirt? But you dont know nothing about it. Miss one week pay'n' and you lose it all."

"I asked him. He said the plan allows. He said . . ."

"It's a buck a month. A buck a month. Ferget it, Anna . . . . Ferget that launderin, too."

Voices of children around the corner lamppost. *"Alley, alley 'ats in free"* came shrill and sweet. Mist tendrils curled closer over the river bluff, heavier fog behind already blotting out the farthest line of clothes.

"Momma, Poppa, why do peoples talk and dogs cant, but last night Shep came back and talked words, yes he did, but I couldn't any more, just woof, woof words. What did I say in woof woof that made Shep mad? He bit me, Poppa, bites all over. Do you see bites on my neck, Poppa?"

"That was a dream, Benjy." Anna said. "Dont you remember Momma came in? I held you and showed you there wasn't no bites and sang you back to sleep."

"But I *saw* Shep. Poppa, Momma, for why do mens give dogs nails in meat, laugh and the dog is bleedin, shaking? A big boy, Antsy down the block, if he sees me he says, 'Hey, shit, come here,' bad words like that, 'I'm going to have me your birdie.' I dont like that big boy, Poppa. For why is he that way? For why is . . . ?"

"You need a muzzle, kid," said Jim, spreading his hand gently over Ben's face to hold it still. "For why'n and for why, huh. How'm *I* supposed to know? Yeah, get eddicated, you get a little respect; know better than to ask fool questions that get lies or nothin for answers . . . Like always happened to me." Rising: "What's it all for, anyhow? . . . A buck a month. Ferget it, Anna." Sharply: "You going to leave this kid out all night in this damp?" taking up Bess and her basket. "Let's eat. Now."

In the square of lemon light from the kitchen window, Anna picked up the laundry basket. The moistness and dimness were all around now. Mazie, slipping out to fetch Anna and Ben, stood transfixed in wonder and fear. Her mother was walking dreamlike round and round the yard, laundry basket on her head, disappearing in and out of the clutching mists; emerging, disappearing; an enchanted Ben following her. Her voice came dreamy and disembodied.

"Yes that's how they carries clothes there, Benjy, basket on their heads, hands on their hips like I cant do. Walking like queens, hoop earrings big as bracelets in their ears. Parrot birds that talk, and flowers bigger than washtubs, all colors and smells."

"Where is it, Momma, where is that place?"

"I dont rightly know. I aint ever been, Benjy. I only saw it in a picture book." She put the basket down, bent to him fiercely: "You read books, you'll know all that. That's what books is: places your body aint ever been, cant ever get to go. Inside people's heads you wouldn't ever know. There's a place here, a liberary where Else gets her reading, where I've been fixin for us to go. They lets you borrow books, picture ones if you cant read yet."

"I want to go see the earrings, talk to the parrot birds that talk. Will the streetcar take us?"

"It's a far place, Benjy. You have to be rich to go, take trains and boats. Or when you grow up you can go, like your Uncle Ralphie, the one you never did see, the one that ships. Boys get to do that," her voice was wistful, "not girls. Ralph's been everyplace. Wonders of the world."

She picked up the basket, set it back on her head, moved back into the dimness. "Wonders of the world." Her voice was dreamy again. "Everything's gone. You cant see 'ary a light. Yes one, so weak and pitiful. You cant see where is our house, where does the bluff end.

A body could end right in the river, not knowin; drift; not fall. As if the world ending right here, we all closed in; just me and the basket and you, Benjy. No, we're not going to fall over the edge, silly . . . Dont it breathe good? . . . fresh? Let's not go in. I declare I feel like a gypsy, wanderin and camping, doing everything outdoors, rolling up in the night too, sleepin out, never going in."

"Lets go in, Momma," pulling at her in sudden fright. "We got to go in. Its suppertime. Don't talk goofy. Mommas always goes in."

Rent week—little in the house to eat besides potatoes and flour—Anna left the baby with Mrs. Kryckszi and wandered the streets with Mazie and Ben and Jimmie, looking for empty lots where dandelions grew. *(The Wheel of Nutrition: One Serving: Green Leafy Vegetable Daily.)* "I hanker for greens," she told them. "We been without a far time now."

She showed Mazie how to look for plants with fresh yellow flowers or just-opening buds, how to select only young, juicy leaves, telling them by their glossy green and tender feel. But the lots were mostly weed, the dandelion heads seedy white, their leaves woody. Though Ben helped too, their paper bags held scarcely a layer.

They wandered on and on. It was a gentle morning; light and warmth flowed in ripples. "I dont remember since when I been out just walkin like this," Anna said. Her lips were parted, her face uplifted to the blue seamless air. Mazie felt the strangeness rising in her mother, not like the sickness strange, something else.

One lot Anna gathered a handful of the seedy puffs and without warning, in one great breath, filled the air with white fluff. "You blew a hundred wishes," crowed

Ben, impressed. "You blew a hundred wishes. What did you wished, Momma?"

"You know if I tell, it cant come true." She bent to her paper bag, blew it full, with a sudden sharp blow popped it; laughed. Jimmie, startled, began to cry. "I'm sorry, Jimmie, I wasn't thinking. We got more paper bags than greens," she explained. "That was to even it up. I guess. You want Momma to carry you awhile? No, dont you dare bust that bag, Ben. We're goin to need it, you'll see. Three bags full."

Another lot, she fell to braiding the stems, while Mazie stood disdainful. "We'll make a chain a block long. Clover's better, but where's any clover?" Ben and even Jimmie ran to get chain makings, carefully running their fingers down the flower stems to the bottom like she showed them to get the longest stems. "Is it a block long yet? Is it a block long yet?" But abruptly she stopped, threw the unfinished chain at Mazie, who threw it back; wrapped Jimmie round and round with it.

They were in a different kind of street now. Lawns, flower beds and borders, children on bikes. Jimmie kept having to be chased after by Mazie and dragged away from other children or things that fascinated him. "This would be a good neighborhood to ask for launderin work," Anna said. A vague shame, a weedy sense of not belonging, of something being wrong about them, stirred uneasy through Mazie. "Momma, I have to pee," Ben said. Anna walked on carelessly, dreamily, ignoring Ben, who gripped tight her skirt with his free hand, his other clutching himself, ignoring Jimmie, who was now petulantly complaining that he was tired tired tired and Mazie was bad and he didn't want to walk any more.

Two girls walking toward them stared and snickered,

turned their heads to look after them. "Ben, get your hand away from yourself," Mazie hissed, and savagely to Jimmie, "If you'll just shut up I'll carry you." For some reason it came out in a whisper.

"Piggyback?"

"If you'll just shut up. *Ma, this isn't the way.*"

"Why dont I have a tricycle?" Ben asked. "Will I get one ever?" and he slowed to stare longingly after an empty one on a lawn, still clinging to Anna's skirt so that, walking on obliviously, her thigh came bared. A woman putting on white gloves came out of a house and smiled at the four of them. Quickly Mazie moved between her and Anna, as if to protect her mother against something.

"Just you keep your face to yourself, lady," Mazie muttered furiously in her head. "Old crummy Nicey Nice.

"Ben!" she ordered in her mother's voice, "dont drag on Momma, walk straight. *Ma, this isn't the way.*"

"That's a fine horse you've got there," the lady said to Jimmie. "Pretty big load, though, aren't you? . . . Are you lost?" she asked Anna.

"Giddyap, Horsie," yelled Jimmie. Mazie galloped ahead, round the corner, out of sight. She shifted Jimmie into her arms, glared at him, said in the earlier savage whisper: "You're a big boy. Big boys walk."

"No. JimJim tired," patting her face lovingly, luxuriously abandoning his body against her. "Swing and sway some more, Madie, swing and sway. Good horsie."

At the end of a cobbly street that had no houses, only high wire fences, they came to a stretch along the river bluff, yellow and green and white with flowers and grass and dandelion glory. A strange heavy fragrance drenched the air. "There's millions here," ex-

ulted Ben after he and Jimmie had relieved themselves.
Mazie was already gathering at the river bluff edge, as
far away from them as she could get. "This was somebody's good yard," Anna said, bending and inspecting.
She put Ben to picking nasturtium leaves—"only the
little ones, Ben, no bigger'n a penny"—then set to
work herself in a swift, practiced rhythm, bending,
loosening, gathering. Bees drowsed there; they had to
be careful. White trumpet-shaped flowers were scattered in the green.

"Catalpa," Anna said suddenly, scooping up a handful of the blooms, "that best smell." She stood up,
pointing to the great tree above. "Mazie, come over.
See you suck honey syrup out of the little end. Taste,
Benjy. Taste, Mazie. Look inside, there's black and
gold and blue markings, beautiful. And the tiny glass
threads standing up as if they was flowers themselves.
Yes, Benjy, they do feel velvet inside. Rub it on your
cheek."

She bent to gather again, went on talking. "One year
when I was high as you, Mazie, we lived a place where
was a tree like that. The leaves aren't rightly out yet,
but when they are, they get the biggest leaves ever you
saw, heart-shaped, and then that tree gets cigars. We'll
come back fall time, you'll see."

Her rhythm had slowed. In between gathering she
sucked the blooms, and Mazie saw that each time before, she drew her breath in deep to smell, deep as if
she had to blow off dandelion heads or pop a paper
bag. A remote, shining look was on her face, as if she
had forgotten them, as if she had become someone
else, was not their mother any more. "Ma, come back,"
Mazie felt like yelling, in rancor, in fear; jumping up,
snapping her fingers into that dreaming face to bring
attention, consciousness of them back, make it the old

known face again. *Snap my fingers.* But her fingers were moving deftly, happily; cool slim mindless tracing down the notched leaves to the roots, the responsive tug, the tiny spurt of juice spilling its spicy smell.

A peace and content began to drowse through her. Bees sounden, she whispered. Sweet smellin. Lady bugs. Butterflies like your dizzy. Unbidden: If you dont look no place, just down, if you dont listen, pretend the trucks and freight noise is 'quipment, it's the farm. Stupid, she chastised herself grievingly, stupid. Who cares about the farm? Who wants to pick stupid weeds? *Snap my fingers in her face.* Loudly: "Ma, dont we have enough yet? *Ma!*"

"Three bags full," said Ben, inspecting.

"I can 'cite that," Jimmie said. "Baa baa black ship, three bags full. Watch how I jump," jumping over and over from a wide step of what had been a house, burned down how long ago.

"Dont we have enough yet?" Mazie repeated.

"You know greens boil down to just nothin," her mother answered. "Yes, I guess that's enough. We'll set awhile. My head is balloony, balloony. Balloony." She staggered, put her arms around Mazie, sang:

> O Shenandoah I love thy daughter
> I'll bring her safe through stormy water

smiled so radiantly, Mazie's heart leapt. Arm in arm, they sat down under the catalpa. That look was on her mother's face again, her eyes so shining and remote. She began stroking Mazie's hair in a kind of languor, a swoon. Gently and absently she stroked.

> Around the springs of gray my wild root weaves,
> Traveler repose and dream among my leaves

her mother sang. A fragile old remembered comfort streamed from the stroking fingers into Mazie, gathered to some shy bliss that shone despairingly over suppurating hurt and want and fear and shamings—the Harm of years. River wind shimmered and burnished the bright grasses, her mother's hand stroked, stroked. Young catalpa leaves overhead quivered and glistened, bright reflected light flowed over, 'lumined their faces. A bee rested on Mazie's leg; magic!—flew away; and a butterfly wavered near, settled, folded its wings, flew again.

I saw a ship a sailing

her mother sang.

A sailing on the sea

Mazie felt the strange happiness in her mother's body, happiness that had nought to do with them, with her; happiness and farness and selfness.

I saw a ship a sailing
And on that ship was me.

The fingers stroked, spun a web, cocooned Mazie into happiness and intactness and selfness. Soft wove the bliss round hurt and fear and want and shame—the old worn fragile bliss, a new frail selfness bliss, healing, transforming. Up from the grasses, from the earth, from the broad tree trunk at their back, latent life streamed and seeded. The air and self shone boundless. Absently, her mother stroked; stroked unfolding, wingedness, boundlessness.

"I'm hungry," Ben said.

"Watch me jump," Jimmie called imperiously. "Momma, Mazie, watch. You're not watching!"

The wind shifted, blew packing house. A tremble of complicity ran through Mazie's body; with both hands she tethered her mother's hand to keep it stroking, stroking. Too late. Something whirred, severed, sank. *Between a breath, between a heartbeat, the weight settled, the bounds reclaimed.*

"I'm watching," Anna called. The mother look was back on her face, the mother alertness, attunement, in her bounded body.

"I didn't think to bring a bite for us, Ben. Wherever is my head these late days? Balloony. Catalpa." She laughed. "Holy Meroly," using an expression they had never heard her use before, "there's nary a shadow. Noontime. And I promised Mis' Kryckszi we'd be back."

Never again, but once, did Mazie see that look—the other look—on her mother's face.

EIGHT

Easeful and huge, the hot July goes through the barefoot weather, the idleness weather. The cramp the
clamp of school released enough, the children of packingtown turn from June wildnesses to deeper, more ancient play.

On the dump, territory is established, shifted, aban-
doned, fought over, combined. Peerers, combers and
excavators go treasure hunting. (They compete with
old men and women looking for covering, furnishings,
sustenance—anything usable, transformable, barter-
able, salable.) Children—already stratified as dummies
in school, condemned as unfit for the worlds of learning, art, imagination, invention—plan, measure, figure,
design, invent, construct, costume themselves, stage
dramas; endlessly—between tasks, errands, smaller
children to be looked after, jobs, dailinesses—live in
passionate absorbed activity, in rapt make-believe.

On the inexhaustible dump strange structures rise:
lookout towers, sets, ships, tents, forts, lean-tos, club-
houses, cities and stores and train tracks, cabooses,
pretend palaces—singularly fitted with once furnishings, never furnishings, or nothing at all.

On the streets, strange vehicles move: a barrel in
which one rolls; cars of apple boxes on wobbling
wheels, steered by broomsticks; axles triumphantly bal-

anced on between bare tires; Pet milk cans strung, raft-
ed together, used as rollers on which one bellyflops
and with swimming motions pushes along; and—favorite mover of all—ridden dreamily or madly to who
knows what fabled destination by the commander at its
steering wheel—sunken rusted Ford front end that
never moves at all.

In the long dusk evenings, the hiding games, the
whirling games begin. Round the lampposts, thick like
the winged things above, children circle and flitter. On
the dump, watch fires burn. And on porches and
stoops, secrets are whispered, songs sung, stories told,
make-believe selves expanded, and dreams float like
iridescent bubbles in the dim enchanted light in the
sifting sad sweet peace.

July—surcease, release, month.

He stands in the doorway and, smiling faintly, says,
"I'm on, Anna. Feeder and utility man; when the run
starts—splitter. Forty-five cents an hour."

"Pritcher up maybe," corrects Kryckszi behind him.
"Long way to splitter."

"No wood-burnin stove for you *this* summer. We're
gettin the gas connected. No launderin someone else's
duds, either. Didn't I tell you we'd manage? Good
times comin, honey, good times."

"Drunk with the job," says Kryckszi, smiling with
his eyes. "Few pennies more pay an hour. You see how
little it takes to make a man happy."

The fireworks go up from their yard too, that Fourth
of July. Mid-afternoon Jim and Will tramp into the
kitchen, their arms bulging triumphantly with packages.

"Bangers and fireworks, rockets and bangers," exults Will.

"Jim, you didn't!" says Anna, paling. "And when Alec said he'd bring some . . . That's like burning money, money we aint got. The rent money?"

"Now honey, I'm earnin, aint I? Independence Day, isn't it, honey? Grand and glorious. We got to celebrate, dont we?"

"What independence *we* got to celebrate?"

"Independent of property, aint we? Got me a woman too independent to kiss her old man, aint I?"

"Will says I'm not getting any firecrackers," burst in Mazie, Annamae trailing behind. "I want my firecrackers. Where's my bangers?"

"Girls don't get firecrackers, do they, Poppa," said Will smugly, rummaging through the packages. "They burn theyselves. Girls and little kids get sparklers."

"Sparklers comin out of your ears tonight, Bigeyes," says Jim expansively, grabbing her as she starts by. "Roman candles, fountains, pinwheels. We're celebratin tonight. Give Poppa a kiss."

"But thats tonight. Poppa, they been scaring the little kids all morning. We got to get them back, dont we, Annamae? Antsie popped a cracker right on Ben's ear, and Annamae's leg is burned. *Let me go, Poppa.* Will's taking them all, dont you take them all, Poppa, he took them all!"

"He's just havin fun. Celebrating. Hold still, squirmy. You're not going noplace. Not till daddy gets his kiss. Holiday day."

"Will!"

"If I hear another scream like that outen you Mazie," said Anna, "you'll have something to scream about. Isn't there enough noise round here already?

. . . Get Ben out from under that table and make yourself useful. I could stand a little helpin. Else and Alec are due any minute. . . . There ought to be a law against them bangers anyway."

A strange sweat of tension is on Anna, her lips moving, trying to remind herself of what is next to do for the holiday dinner. She does not notice Ben huddling back under the kitchen table, holding his ears, rocking and rocking. Up on the roof, Mazie and Annamae throw ineffectual lit matches down when the boys hove into sight, Jimmie shadowing Will and Smoky and Antsie in delighted terror. Out in the back yard, where Jim and Kryckszi and Alec pitch horseshoes, Else soothes Bess, who starts at every bang.

Now at last, in the warm darkness, plumes of light arise. Children run with sparklers, Jimmie darting after, cupping his hands to catch the spray. Alex and Jim and Will in glory select, set up, light fireworks. Puffs and bursts and sprays.

"Look, we making stars," Ben greets each fountain, skyrocket, roman candle, "we makin stars. What's next, Poppa?" Jeff makes a chant of it, moving his body in time. "Look look! We makin stars. Dance till you out, stars, dance till you out."

"Fallin and dancing," Ben chants back, "Fallin and dancing. Poppa, what's next? Dance till you out." Annamae and Jimmie chorus along: "Stars. Stars. Fallin and dancin. Dance till you out. You out. You out. You out."

All over the sky, echoings, flowerings. Sizzles. Stems of flame, tendrils coiling, climbing. Anna—gratefully off her feet for the first time in that long day—sitting and watching, forgets the grudging rankle at the needed money thrown away, folds herself into the beauty and singing and everyone's happiness. But her

heart yearns over Mazie, sullenly apart on the roof, refusing to touch the fireworks, to be part of the celebra-
tion.

(Only it excites Mazie so, the stems and jettings of
light, the momentary lit faces, the chanting. And now
the great pure ball of light rising over the dark shoulders of bluff.)

"Stars. Stars. Dance till you out."

Kryckszi takes his violin and in the moon dappled
darkness makes a tune of it. Else and Jim, Alex and
Mis' Kryckszi dance.

"Fallin and dancin. Dance till you out." The head-
light of a train weaves and flickers through the dark
bluffs across the silvered river, is lost in distance with
its high forlorn flickering whistle.

"Stars. Stars."

O it's us again, thinks Mazie, it's us. Then in
clenching fear: Now something bad's going to have to
happen. Again.

But it is easier for a while. The old Anna back in
command, reclaimed, wholly given over; the house
once more orderly. Secretly the first insurance pay-
ments are made; secretly Jim looks for a secondhand
sewing machine for Anna. The garden spews forth
puny and pale, gains confidence, begins to garnish the
table. Expeditions are for berry picking now as well as
for greens, one lot where the brambles grow.

One afternoon Anna cleans up the kids and brings
them to her Temple of Learning. A squat dirty convert-
ed storefront (good enough for packingtown, they
said) shelved with opiates and trash and marvels (from
which most of the children are already turned in
outraged self-respect, for is it not through books, the
printed word, or so it seemed, that they had been

judged poor learners, dumb dumb dumb? Told: what is in us has nothing to do with you).

But marvels to Anna *(places your body aint ever been, cant ever get to go; inside people's heads; things you wouldn't never know);* keys, too, in that door to a better life on which opportunity would knock some day. She took out a library card for each. Only Ben pored over his (picture) books. Mazie's and Will's lay untouched. For how onceuponatime and they-livedveryhappyeverafter fairy tales which the librarian had selected for Mazie? how adventure and magic books she had picked for Will, when there is the adventure and fairy ground of dump and city; the conjurer magic of a shining screen in darkness Saturdays.

(Already the conjurer is working spells on Anna's children. Subtly into waking and dreaming, into imagination and everyday doings and play, shaping, altering them. Even outwardly: Will's eyes are narrowed now, his mouth drawn up at the corner, his walk—when he remembers—loose; for the rest of his life he will grin crooked: Bill Hart.)

Sometimes Will or Mazie bring home finds from the dump. A rusted waffle iron, clothespins, blackened forks and spoons, coils from a crystal radio set, a solderable pot. Once a fought-over chair—rung and leg gone. On the high window sill in the kitchen, along with a fragment of prism, is an indigo-blue ink bottle soaked and scrubbed a dozen times to get the glass clear—beautiful to Anna for the light shining through. A saucer—its cracks adding a ghost mysteriousness to its landscape—snowy mountain, fir trees, clouds, tiny burdened Japanese figures toiling across a red curved bridge—is kept in the center of the kitchen table for all to marvel at.

Stealthily Mazie and Will stalk the ice trucks and

wagons for falling slivers to trickle down their throats; for handfuls that can be scooped up while the iceman delivers his ice. Lithe and graceful, they learn to hitch onto the moving trucks, shove over chips, sometimes a whole ice block onto waiting hands. (But Mazie is not long among them. One time a chant starts up:

> Girl go to London, go to France
> Evrybody sees your pants
> Girl shimmy, shimmy shimmyhigh
> Evrybody sees your pie

and after that shame and self consciousness make her body awkward. Twice she misses, almost goes under the wheels. No more for her that lithe joy, that sense of power.)

On the dump there is Jinella's tent, Jinella's mansion, Jinella's roadhouse, Jinella's pagan island, Jinella's palace, whatever Jinella wills it to be that day. Flattened tin cans, the labels torn off to show the flashing silver, are strung between beads and buttons to make the shimmering, showy entrance curtains. Here sometimes, in humble capacity, Mazie is admitted—*if* she brings something for the gunny sack. The gunny sack into which the curtains and tent themselves go when Jinella must go and which is stuffed with "properties": blond wood-shaving curls, moldering hats, raggy teddies, torn lace curtains (for trains and wedding dresses), fringes, tassels, stubs of lipstick, wrecks of high-heeled shoes and boots, lavish jewelry Tiffany would never recognize: greening curtain rings, feathers, fish lures, dress beadings, glass bits, shiny coils and machinery parts. Anything that dangles, jangles, bangles, spangles.

Twelve-year-old Jinella's text: the movies, selected.

Ones Mazie, the late-come country novice, has never seen. *Sheik of Araby. Broken Blossoms. Slave of Love. She Stopped at Nothing. The Fast Life. The Easiest Way.*

Luxuriously on her rug, pretend silk slinking and slithering on her body, turbanned, puffing her long pretend cigarette: Say vamp me, vamp me. I'm Nazimova. Take me to the roadhouse, I want to make whoopee. Hotcha. Never never never. O my gigolo, my gigolo. A moment of ecstasy, a lifetime of regret.

And once alone, smelling sweet of Blue Waltz and moist flesh, her arms tight around Mazie, passionately: whisper to me: Jeannine my queen of lilac time. Jeannine I dream of lilac time. Whisper it. Kiss me. Forever, forever never to part, my pagan love.

On the stoop, evenings Ben imparts his terrible texts to Jimmie:

> Skinny, skinny, run for your life,
> Here comes fatty with a butcher knife.

> Ladybug, ladybug, fly away home,
> Your house is on fire, your children all gone.

> You're it and got a fit,
> Never, never get over it.

> Never know how to get over it.

Plaintively, as if he understands its meaning:

> Ol' clothes to sell, ol' clothes to sell,
> If *I* had as much money as I could tell
> I never would cry ol' clothes to sell.

And desolately:

> Mother, Mother, I am sick.
> Call the doctor quick, quick, quick.
> Doctor, Doctor, will I die?

> Yes. You will. And so shall I.

Mazie, slackly sitting, suddenly *listens,* shudders and gathers them both to her, saying firmly: We're going to sing Hoopde Dooden Do Barney Google with the Googlygoogly Eyes I'm Dreamin Now of Hally; Pop, tell Ben and Jimmie when you were little. *But the day at Cudahy's has thieved Pop's text*—his mouth open, he sleeps the sleep of exhaustion. And when Anna comes out, her apron front still wet from doing dishes, it is too late for texts—the children's eyes droop.

In the dim enchanted light, in the sifting sad sweet peace of summer evening.

And now the dog days are here, the white fierce heat throbbing, when breathing is the drawing in of a scorching flame and the pavement on the bare feet of the children is a sear; when the very young and the very old sicken and die, and the stench cooking down into the pavements and the oven houses throbs like a great wave of vomit in the air.

There in the packing houses the men and women somehow toil through. Standing there, the one motion all day, their clothes salty with sweat, or walking in and out of the cooler till the cold is a fever and the heat a chill, and the stink bellying up from the blood house and casings forces the beginning of a vomit, even on those who boasted they hadn't a smeller any more.

Oh yes, the heavy air clamps down like a coffin lid over the throbbing streets, on the thin cries of babies and the querulous voices of the old, and a sound of breathing hoarse and strained, of breathing feeble and labored goes up; and from beneath the glisten of sweat on a thousand brows, a mocking bitterness in old old words: is it hot enough for you? in a dozen dialects, is it hot enough, hot enough, hot enough for you?

Nights, sleepless nights. Sad rustle of leaves in the unmoving trees and the creak of bedsprings as the sleepless ones toss.

"How much longer can it last, Jim?" asks Anna. "Six days not down to a hundred *once*. The kids cant stand it."

"Just the kids? . . . Whew, if I could get just one cool breath. You'd think we'd get a little wind out the window."

"Momma, why cant I sleep?"

Will is sleeping. Will is lying out on his mattress in the yard, under the bleared stars and the unmoving trees, dreaming of movies, of the shining screen in the darkness and the gallop, gallop of cowboy horses. Waking to a whining mosquito sting, he stares into the sky and tries to breathe and feels as if a lasso is looped tight around his chest a hundred times. Only the trees so high and the cool far stars make him remember his horde of findings he will sell to Curly tomorrow who will sell it to the junkman, and the worms he and Smoky will dig by the river to sell; and his hand curves to the imaginary ball he will buy with his money, and he smiles, tosses restlessly awhile and sleeps.

"Momma, why cant I sleep?"

In the little room the heat is entombed deathly still and unmoving, sweat almost breaks out on the walls,

and the slit of window is like a hungry mouth that sti-
fled, opens to suck in the air. Jimmie is moaning,
scratching his mosquito bites, doing a dance on the
mattress with his body, waking and sleeping again,
waking and sleeping; and Mazie wakes from terrible
lands of dream to feel the heavy heat still there.

Outside it is better, dragging her quilt out besides
Will, but the dark mysterious night scares her and the
mosquitos bite worse and worse and lying there awake
she is thinking of the smoke and fires curling up
around the lady in that movie tied there to the stake,
she can hear in her ears the crackling, hot hot, and she
is thinking of Erina, Erina of the twisted jerking body
and the fits who dragged away Mazie's findings from
the dump and moaned Suffer little children the Bible
says Children suffer suffer. Her body is becoming Erina's body; she *is* Erina, stump arm ending in a little
knob, the spasm walk, the drool. Slapping at a
mosquito, missing, then it splotching squishy under her
hand, a lot of blood, she could see it in the vague light,
blood; dragging her quilt back in again.

"Momma, why cant I sleep?"

Ben is sick, Ben cant sleep, Ben is saying, Momma,
why cant I sleep, Momma, only he can't remember
whether he is saying it or not and the air chokes thick
in his nostrils, sits humping up and down on his chest.
Fast fast fast goes his heart, where is it going, it will
run out of him, run away. There is a big fire somewhere, that is what is making it hot, somebody making
a fire or it was a fire and he is in the stove, black all
around like something burned.

"Momma, why cant I sleep?"

Down the street they are all lying together, Jeff and
Buford and B.G. and Ellis on one great tick, and they
sleep with delicate sharp breaths; and farther down old

lady Dykstra is breathing hoarse and strained, her mouth open, her heart flaying and jumping, and faint and far are babies crying, well babies, sick babies.

The ice is melting in the iceboxes faster and faster, the melting that is the women's despair. Cattle trucks are rattling on the spoke roads to the slaughter houses, thick-packed lambs and calves and hogs snuffling and swaying and stamping, cattle lowing plaintively. Far off the freight trains make a sleepy sound; then faster louder faster.

Gurgle gurgle, the river quiet and secret, the weak soiled vapor shawl, a few men standing and fishing. And for miles and miles the corn in white gold stillness stiff and parched in black baked earth in the black baked night.

"Momma, why cant I sleep?"

Thoughts of death, in this still heat Mazie waking again and thinking thoughts of death, doctor. doctor will I die yes you *will* and so shall I, the sad rustle of the leaves in the trees with drier sound of coming fall.

"Momma." Crying. And momma is coming and wrings out a towel; Ben, Benjy; will she have to take him to the clinic? Thank God Bessie is a baby and sleeps, Bessie is alright. There, Ben, momma has helped the rash, if I hold and fan you and we set outside, will it help you catch your breath?

"Momma, I wish it was mornin."

The fire is coming into the sky, the still still fire, and suddenly it has blazed up, the fetid sun, the red red sun. And the dew which is the tears the sweat of the night is vanished.

Jim and Anna are up, then Jimmie and Bess. Ben is sleeping now and Mazie is sleeping, no need to wake them, and Will is up, secretly shuffling things under his bed.

"Will you get it for me today, my 'monica?" begs Jimmie as he trundles down the street with his father. "Tonight will you bring it, tonight?"

"You going to have a harp, make music for us all maybe?" asks Mr. Kryckszi, joining Jim. "Stay out of the sun today, little Jim. Keep breath to blow strong." . . . Looking at its festering orange straight ahead. To Jim: "Not good. A hundred and ten in kill room, more in casings today, you see. Oven. Maybe already. Afraid for Marsalek, for Mary. I talk to Misho, to Huff, to Slim. We have to slow it, I tell them, get break too. Misho talk for us to Wild Man Ed." Shaking his head: "No good."

"That prick Ed," says Jim. "How else'd he make straw boss?"

"Wild Man Ed say Bull Young tell him is no sweat. We bunch lazies."

"Lazies! That pusher. Beedo* hisself, in person." They are over the viaduct now.

"You see, a hundred and ten—maybe hotter."

"Be hell," says Jim, looking down at the plant, "be Hell."

Hell.

Choreographed by Beedo, the B system, speed-up stopwatch, convey. Music by rasp crash screech knock steamhiss thud machinedrum. Abandon self, all ye who enter here. Become component part, geared, meshed, timed, controlled.

Hell. Figures half-seen through hissing vapor, live steam cloud from great scalding vats. Hogs dangling, dancing along the convey, 300, 350 an hour; Mary running running along the rickety platform to keep up, stamping, stamping the hides. To the shuddering drum

*Beedo: A speed-up system of the 1920's.

of the skull crush machine, in the spectral vapor clouds, everyone the same motion all the hours through: Kryckszi lifting his cleaver, the one powerful stroke; long continuous arm swirl of the rippers, gut pullers; Marsalek pulling leaf lard, already faint in the sweated heat, breathing with open mouth.

Breathing with open mouth, the young girls and women in Casings, where men will not work. Year-round breathing with open mouth, learning to pant shallow to endure the excrement reek of offal, the smothering stench from the blood house below. Windowless: bleared dank light. Clawing dinning jutting gnashing noises, so overweening that only at scream pitch can the human voice be heard. Heat of hell year round, for low on their heads from the lowering ceiling, the plant's steam machinery. Incessant slobber down of its oil and scalding water onto their rubber caps, into their rubber galoshes. O feet always doubly in water—inside boots, outside boots. Running water overflow from casings wash. Spurting steam geysers. Slippery uncertain footing on the slimy platform. Treacherous sudden torrents swirling (the strong hose trying to wash down the blood, the oil, the offal, the slime). And over and over, the one constant motion—ruffle fat pullers, pluck separators, bladder, kidney, bung, small and middle gut cutters, cleaners, trimmers, slimers, flooders, inflators—*meshed, geared*.

Geared, meshed: the kill room: knockers, shacklers, pritcher-uppers, stickers, headers, rippers, leg breakers, breast and aitch sawyers, caul pullers, fell cutters, rumpers, splitters, vat dippers, skinners, gutters, pluckers.

Ice hell. Coolers; freezers. Pork trim: bone chill damp even in sweaters and overshoes; hands always in icy water, slippery knives, the beedo piece work speed—safety signs a mockery.

—All through the jumble of buildings old and buildings new; of pens, walkways, slippery stairs, overhead chutes, conveys, steam pipes; of death, dismemberment and vanishing entire for harmless creatures meek and mild, frisky, wild—Hell.

Today—the fifth day of hell-heat added—104° outside, 112° in casings. Seven o'clock.

Ooh it's so hot, Mazie waking up feeling charred and smoldering, and going into the kitchen, her legs scabby and blood-splotched with open mosquito sores scratched too much, and Bess cooing at her, Ben up and in a chair, his eyes looking too big and too sick.

Not hungry. Her head hurting and hurting. Having to help pit and peel the canning apples and peaches.

"Havent I done enough, Ma? Cant I go out and play? It's too hot in here."

"If you get back 'fore noon," Anna says, thinking: Better now before the sun's really up. "This cannin's got to get done today."

But it was even hotter outside. The sun burned on her back, but her head didnt hurt so much. Only the light seemed fire.

Annamae ran out when she saw her. "What we gonna do today?" Mazie asked listlessly.

"The findins! There was new things dumped yestidday. Maybe we'll pass a ice truck or wagon."

No trucks; the streets glittered empty like in a dream. And there was nothing really new on the dump. It smelled sewer, smelled garbage, smelled crap 'cept right at the river-bluff edge. Grubbing, Mazie found a torn magazine with funny words—a furrin language, painting pictures, different colors and patterns. "Wallpaper for our dollhouse, it'll make wallpaper." But out of one of the pages, a little girl's eyes stared at her, big eyes, black, almost holes, from her face lots and lots of lines going all kinds of ways, so much lines you couldn't look at them all but you had to try while your head got dizzier and dizzier. And scareder. It was something like you, like something . . .

Mazie tore the little girl and the scary lines into teeny kite bits but didn't have any breath to blow them; lay down on her belly looking down over the bluff and fluttered them away instead. No cool wind came up. The tracks and trains flashed hot; the river flashed too though a dirty haze lay on it as if it were too lazy to move.

"My momma don't let me go down by the river," she told Annamae. "Will your momma? She says bad people's there that hurts girls." She grubbed with one hand for what turned out to be an old doorknob to throw down to where she couldn't go. It landed right on the open gondola of a sluggish freight train. All the way to California, she thought.

There was Will, going down the road with Smoky. "Where you going?" she hailed, scrambling after though getting up so fast made her head pound and be dizzier.

"No place."

"Then I'm going too."

"Oh no you aint. We dont want no tattletale girls."

"I am too goin."

"Oh no you aint. Run, Smoke, run," scooping a handful of pebbles and dirt to fling at her.

She chased them a block, but fell and skinned her knee and they were out of sight. Where the pebbles hit, it stung and prickled like the mosquito bites. She scratched them all open again, sucked at one on her arm, for she was so thirsty, so thirsty.

The sun seemed to have a big tongue that was licking her back and her head hurted worse and worse and the lines going all directions round and round. Everything looked glassy and wavy.

Jinella was in her tent. Mazie stood outside the glittering curtains. Katie and Char were fanning her; Jinella was Queen Tut or Nazimova, lying on her rug, pretend smoking. "Googly," she said languidly, seeing Mazie. "Gwan and melt. We dont want any Miss Uglys around . . . Unless you got ice." Yesterday she had passed their house when Mazie was holding Ben. "Fishface," she had said coolly, cruelly to Ben, "Whyn't you close your mouth, Fishface?"

Miss Ugly!

Annamae was still scrabbling in the pile for stuff. Ellie was there, eating a huge peach. "My grandma gave it so I wouldnt make noise. She's sick, maybe she'll die." Proffering a bite.

"My little brother's real sick too," said Mazie, wishing she could add self-importantly: he may get dead too. (I dont mean it, Benjy.) "Let's go look for a ice wagon."

"No, it's lucky here," objected Annamae. Her face was flushed. "See?" Holding up a tiny round mirror.

"That's mine," lied Mazie, thinking of Jinella. "I put it there and now you took it. Give it back."

"It's not either yours. I took it out of a compact, didnt I, Ellie? it was all moldy and greeny, ughy ughy, and I had to clean it, didn't I?"

"Give it to me," swiping for Annamae's hand. "Alright, dont. I dont want to play anyway."

Erina was coming. Wavering in the heat waves,

dragging along, jerking funny; skinny with her bones sticking out like great knobs and the tiny arm stub that hung down and ended in a knob. Coming closer, coming right to them. Flickering out her faded tongue and the spit slobbering down. "Pennies," she said. "Little girls, do you have any pennies? For ice cream. It hurts. Pennies."

"I dont have none," faltered Mazie, backing toward Ellie and Annamae, who shook their heads mutely to signify that they didn't have any either; fascinatedly unable to look away from the running sores on her legs and her pitiful arm.

"What you think you're staring at?" advancing ferociously as they kept backing. "Pfeh," she spit.

Ellie surrendered what was left of the peach to Erina. There was no place but the river-cliff edge behind.

"I'll go home and ask a penny," said Annamae.

"Me too," said Ellie.

"Payday my papa buys us Eskimo pies," said Mazie faintly. "I'll give you mine, Erina."

"Now," said Erina. "I'm burnin. God is looking at you. That is his burning eye up there."

She will push me over the cliff, thought Mazie. I have to run quick like Annamae, like Ellie. But it was a bad dream where you couldn't move. The lines going dizzy.

"The devil is roasting us today; the devil is frying us, like in hell. For our sins." Erina's breath was in Mazie's face; Mazie saw how the pus oozed from her eyes, stuck on her eyelashes; weed stickers—maybe lice—in her hair. *Go away, Erina; it's so hot and you are wavy like everything else. Last night I was your body, I was you. Go away.* "Maybe my momma will give a penny."

"It hurts inside," Erina said, crying and slobbering.

"Hold me so it dont hurt." She put her one arm around Mazie, who shuddered violently. "I'm ugly," Erina sobbed. "God made me like this." Crouching down at Mazie's feet.

(Miss Ugly). Mazie sank resistless down on the cracked earth beside her; its heat came up in waves too, like the glassy waves she could see in the air. "Shall I go look for a ice truck and steal you some ice, Erina?"

"Shall we pray?" asked Erina. "I pray but God dont make me better and Pa and Tammysue socks me 'cause it means I was sinning too bad to get forgiven. Do you sin, little girl?"

"I'm big," said Mazie. "I'm going to be nine, almost as old as you, Erina," and began to grub in the hot stiff soil at the half-decayed rags in it.

"Watch for my bird," said Erina, "Watch for its little bones. It was deaded and I put it in the ground there and blessed it, but when I got back it was on top half et with worms and crawly things and stinky and I had to cover it back. Bones now." Swallowing thirstily and slobbering. "When you die your soul goes to hell or heaven but your body gets et and stinks."

"That's a song," said Mazie, a sick-happy feeling to be with Erina, to listen to Erina, rising in her. "The worms go in and the worms go out and they eat up all of your chin and mouth."

"Watch for the little ants," said Erina. "Dont hurt their houses. They have to hurry and work so hard and carry heavy things and I sees them carry each other sometime."

Erina looked really sick; her eyes were like that little girl's in the painting-picture, black holes. What Mazie had thought was dirt on her cheek was bad bruises. Was she going to get a fit? "Erina," she said gently,

"Jinella has lemon cream soda in her tent. I'll ask will she give some."

"Jinella!" said Erina. She smoothed and gentled her little stub arm and it tried to rise up as if to gentle her back. "When she sees me she says here comes freak show, stink show, Miss Sewer from shantylicetown." Her face quivered. "Suffer little children the Bible says."

"Rest, Erina. I'll find you some ice quick, or ice cream or another peach or lemon cream."

Jinella and Katie and Char were gone; the tent and the clinky glittery curtains and the dress-up bag, gone. Erina was gone too, weaving toward the viaduct under where shantytown was. Mazie wanted to fall and push herself along on her belly after her. Flat like a caterpillar, not wavy like a worm or jumpy like a grasshopper. Crawl flat on her belly. Not have to walk. Her head throbbed biggern the whole world and like all her blood was boiling up into it, percolating. She walked slow as she could, but fell. It was the sole of her shoe come loose and flapping made her stumble: *I told you I didnt want to have to wear shoes today, Ma!* She worked them off, but the ground frizzled and she had to put them back on.

She wanted to cry but she did not know what about. She wanted to hear Erina talk—but not have to look at her. She felt sick and mean and screamy, and sad and mad and bad. Her throat swallowed and swallowed with nothing in it to swallow, so dry, sticking together, hurting. Last night she dreamed she swung the Big Dipper round and round and drank the night with the ice stars in it. She could have told Erina that, Erina would have listened and not laughed. Stars are fire, not ice—stars are suns, she reminded herself scornfully. Old Man Caldwell. Tied to the stake, flames curling round her feet and up toward her belly, everybody laughing, Miss Ugly. Yes, she was. She sat down on the curb and looked at her burning feet. She wanted to go to the catalpa place and sit under that tree; or down to the river where she had never been and Will got to go; it would be cool with ice like night in God's Dipper.

A lady in a car stopping at the corner held a handkerchief to her nose, real delicate. Mazie picked up a corncob from the gutter and threw it hard at the car.

Right by the house, in the shade, Jimmie and Jeff and Ben were playing. Jeff held a strange stringed instrument his brothers had made for him, a cigarbox body with a long slab of wood jutting out; strung on it a dozen kinds of strings and wires. With it he made a jangling, and sang in an unearthly voice. Jimmie sang too, rocking a half of a Quaker Oats round cereal box cut the long way; in it was a stick wrapped round with rags in the semblance of a doll. Ben, for all the heat swathed in a blanket, sat gravely watching and rocking himself in time.

"Fishface," she heard herself saying in Jinella's inflections, "why don't you close your mouth, fishface? . . . My cradle," swooping down, "my own cradle I made."

"It's to rock baby," pleaded Jimmy. "We're rocking baby to sleep."

". . . playing . . . house," Ben explained, breathing loud between each word.

"You never asked could you have it. And there goes your baby," swinging it out far as she could into the yard.

"You . . . hurted . . . her," Ben said accusingly, his eyes, bigger than ever with their illness, filling with tears.

But she was in the kitchen, tears, and meanness

fighting in her, banging the door after her right into wailing Jimmie's face.

"Now what's the matter?" Anna asked, her head bobbing over the steaming kettles. "Oh its you. Now what trouble you been up to?"

"She tooked it away, she threw it away," wailed Jimmie louder and louder.

"Hush, you, hush. Don't you know Bess is finally sleepin and you mustnt make noise?" Opening the door to let him in. *"What* did she take away?"

"My cradle," defended Mazie, "the one I made."

"She took our baby too. She tooked it and threw it far away."

"By . . . the cliff." Ben toiled in. He was crying. "You're bad, Sistie."

"Did you go hunt for it, Ben?" Anna splashed her spoon into the kettle she was stirring, "when you knew you arent to move at all, and I just let you out if you'd set still?" To Mazie: "Miserable child! Look what you've done. He wasnt to move."

"I didnt know he would go lookin for it," Mazie said. "And it was my cradle, wasnt it, my very own I made?"

"Wash your hands—it wouldn't hurt your face none either—and get a apron on," Anna commanded, wringing a cloth for Ben's head, taking him on her lap and fanning him. "You knowed we have to get this cannin done, I'm gettin no place fast between watchin Jimmie and tendin Ben and baby. We got to fix a bite too."

"Why is it always me that has to help? How come Will gets to play?"

"Willies a boy."

"Why couldn't *I* get borned a boy?"

"You get to play enough," Anna said shortly. *(Just seems the devil's got into her.)*

"Don't you move now," settling Ben on the couch; shaving the paraffin into a pan to melt; and going back to stirring the bubbling mass of jelly. If this heat keeps up, I'll just melt, she thought, drop and melt all over. They wont know which is paraffin and which is me. . . . If only Benjy dont get so bad I have to fetch him to the clinic.

Mazie was yanking her skirt, her face white, in her hand an empty bottle. "Somebody spillded it," she shrieked, "somebody spillded my perfume I made. My very own perfume."

"Shhhhh. It was me. How should I a-known it was supposed to be perfume you wanted to save? It was dirty-smelly stuff stuck in the cupboard where it didn't belong."

"It was perfume. I made it out of flower leaves. You put them in a bottle and cork it and leave it. It was for Jinella and I never get a nickel to buy her Blue Waltz and now I haven't any perfume."

"Well there's more makings where that came from. And next time dont keep it where it dont belong."

Shrieking again: "I dont *have* no place. If I'd kept it in the bedroom Jimmie woulda been into it, or maybe Will." Violently: *"Why dont I have no place?"*

"Hush, I said. That's enough outen you. You wake baby and see what you'll get. Start to stirrin now . . . Thoughtfully: Maybe I can make a place for you on a shelf somewhere soon as I get some time. Dont see why not."

But Mazie was gone.

"Come back," yelled Anna out the screen door, "come back right this minute or you'll get a whoppin."

Now, who's wakin baby? she asked herself. Uncomfortably: She oughtn't to be out in that sun without a hat . . . And she *doesn't* have a place for her things.

"Ben!" She hears the loud rattling of his breath, turns. He points at the opening door. Mazie crawls in, puts her arms around her mother's legs and howls.

"What's the matter, sweetheart?" Helping her up.

"I dont know. My head, Momma. I dont know."

Falling. Fainting.

"Sistie! Maaaaaaa!" begs Ben, baaing like a sheep. He runs with his fan and water.

Overhead the inflamed sun glares in an inflamed sky. Twelve o'clock noon. 106°.

"Slow it," Kryckszi sends the message to Misho, to Huff, to Ella. "We got to slow it."

The fifteen-minute lunch break goes like nothing. Those who (against the rules) had crowded into the cooler or the chill damp of pork trim to eat their lunch find their names up on the bulletin board with fines posted against them. *(Who ratted?)* Those who had sluiced themselves down with the hoses in the yards for momentary relief (also against the rules) suffer other punishment. Their clothes will not dry; cling; tighten; become portable sweat baths as they work. Aitch-sawyer Crowley, the venerable, faints. Prostration. By word or gesture or look of the eye, the message goes out in each department: spell Marsalek; spell Lena; spell Laurett; spell Salvatore: however possible, spell, protect those known near their limit of endurance.

In Casings it is 110°. A steam kettle, thinks Ella, who had a need to put things into words, a steam kettle, and in a litany: *steamed, boiled, broiled, fried, cooked; steamed, boiled, broiled, fried, cooked.* Tony,

Smoky's older brother, lugging his hand truck from fire to chill to fire (casings to cooler to casings) fans the cooler door open for the women as long as he dares. Each time (the hands never ceasing their motions) even those too far away for relief turn their heads in unison toward the second's different air, flare their nostrils, gulp with open mouths. The stench is vomit-making as never before. The fat and plucks, the bladders and kidneys and bungs and guts, gone soft and spongy in the heat, perversely resist being trimmed, separated, deslimed; demand closer concentration than ever, extra speed. A hysterical, helpless laughter starts up. Indeed they are in hell; indeed they are the damned. *Steamed boiled broiled fried cooked. Geared, meshed.*

In the hog room, 108°. Kerchiefs, bound around foreheads to keep the salt sweat from running down into eyes and blinding, become saturated; each works in a rain of stinging sweat. Almost the steam from the vats seems cloud-cool, pure, by contrast. Marsalek falls. A heart attack. (Is carried away, docked, charged for the company ambulance.) Other hearts pound near to bursting. Relentless, the convey paces on.

Slow it, we got to slow it.

Is it a dream, is it delirium? Arms lifted to their motion *(geared, meshed)* have nothing to move for. The hog has been split, has been stamped—yet still dangles; the leaf lard, the guts, have been pulled, yet no new carcass is instantly in place to be worked on. Has life suspended, are they dead? The skull-crush machine still stomping down, sprays out its bone bits in answer. "Fined, fined for carelessness," yells Bull Young. "What jammed the convey?"—turning instinctively toward Kryckszi.

At that moment in Casings, as if to demonstrate that

there is a mightier heat, a higher superior heat, the main steam pipe breaks open, and hissing live steam in a magnificent plume, in a great boiling roll, takes over. Peg and Andra and Philomena and Cleola directly underneath, fall and writhe in their crinkling skins, their sudden juices. Lena, pregnant, faints. Laurett trying to run, slips on the slimy platform. Others tangle over her, try to rise, to help each other up. Ella, already at the work of calming, of rescue, thinks through her own pain: steamed boiled broiled cooked *scalded,* I forgot *scalded.*

When the door to the hog room, always kept closed against the Casings stench, the Casings heat, is flung open, the steam boils in so triumphantly, weds with the hog-vat vapors to create such vast clouds, such condensation, the running scalded figures of horror (human? women?) seem disembodied flickering shadows gesturing mutely back to whence they have fled. "Stay where you are," yells Bull. "Carelessness. Nobody's gettin away with nothin. You'll be docked for every second you aint workin. And fined for carelessness."

Already some are in casings, helping. Carrying Lena out of the scalding fog, Jim sees plastered onto her swollen belly the SAFETY sign torn from the wall by the first steam gust.

Three o'clock. 107°.

Old Mrs. Dykstra cries out once into the heavy air, gasps and breathes no more. Overhead, blown eggshell doves she has made old-country style with wings and tail of white pleated paper, bob three times—and still.

Will and Smoky turn from the river for the steep climb toward home, their dream of pockets of jingle money from juicy fishing worms, defeated by the impermeable armor of the sun-hardened shore. Outside the Palace, they stare at movie stills. "A crook picture," Will says longingly. But nowhere, nowhere that nickel.

On her way home—where she will be beaten for having been gone, for having been born, for having been born crippled and epileptic, for being one more mouth to feed and because out of sheer nervousness and exhaustion there is a need for someone to beat— Erina no longer feels heat or thirst or the gnawing in her belly. On a tin-can roof of one of the shacks some-one has set a pan of shining water where cat and dog cannot reach it, and a bird is bathing itself, fluttering its wings in delight. In its tiny spray that the sun rainbows, Erina stands motionless, feeling in herself the shining, the fluttering happiness. The thigh-high weeds are powdered white with dust. When the bird is done, she climbs to drink of the water in which feathers float, takes and holds one to dry in the furnace air, turns and smoothes it over and over against her bruised cheek. The vast winds of fit may blow any minute; the shameful trembling and great darkness begin, but she walks now in the fluttering shining and the peace.

In her secret place, the shelter under the porch stoop, Jinella hides and is ill. "Too hot," she whispers, "too hot," turning her head from side to side as if that would fan coolness. How rosy she is from the heat, how creamy. Droplets of sweat glow like moonstones on her flawless skin.

"Gertrude," her mother calls, "Gertrude. I seen you come." Ugly, the Polish, the foreigner sound of her mother's voice. Ugly what waits upstairs. Spiders of heat waver through the splintered steps onto her red knuckled hands with their broken fingernails. Spasmodically Jinella folds their shame into her skirt. Ugly. Slender white fingers with talon fingernails float unattainable in the dust mote air. Ugly, I'm ugly.

"Gertrude," her mother calls again, "work waiting. You do before you have to go Mirkas or you get whipping. You be late Mirkas, you get whipping. . . . Gertrude!" In an hour she must go to her aunt's diner, be among thick crowded, guttural-voiced, sweating working men; plunge her hands into scalding reddening water, be the slavey, scrub greasy pots and dishes and counter tops. "Hot, it's so hot," fanning her head from side to side. "I'm sick, Ma. I cant do nothin." Sick with the feverish heat; sick with an older feverish longing, unutterable, to be other than she is; to be otherwhere than she is—places spacious and elegant, idle and served and cool. *Slave of Desire. Forbidden Paradise.* Not shamed and shameful, not judged and condemned. "Classy, I want to be classy," she whispers.

"Gertrude," her mother yells, "Gertrude Skolnick. Now! *Wstawach!*" *Human Wreckage.* She starts up the stairs.

In the humid kitchen, Anna works on alone. Mazie lies swathed in sweated sleep in the baking bedroom. Jimmie and Jeff sleep under the kitchen table, their exhausted bodies, their hair damp and clinging to their perspiring heads, giving them the look of drowned children. Ben lies in sleep or in a sleep of swoon, his poor heaving chest laboring on at its breathing. Bess has subsided in her basket on a chair where, if she frets, Anna can sprinkle her with water or try to ease the heat rash by sponging. The last batch of jelly is on the stove. Between stirring and skimming, and changing the wet packs on Ben, Anna peels and cuts the canning peaches—two more lugs to go. If only all will sleep awhile. She begins to sing softly—*I saw a ship a-sailing, a-sailing on the sea*—it clears her head. The drone of fruit flies and Ben's rusty breathing are very loud in the unmoving, heavy air. Bess begins to fuss again. *There, there, Bessie, there, there,* stopping to sponge down the oozing sores on the tiny body. *There.* Skim, stir; sprinkle Bess; pit, peel and cut; sponge; skim, stir. Any second the jelly will be right and must not wait. Shall she wake up Jimmie and ask him to blow a feather to keep Bess quiet? No, he'll wake cranky, he's just a baby hisself, let him sleep. Skim, stir; sprinkle; change the wet packs on Ben; pit, peel and cut; sponge. This time it does not soothe—Bess stiffens her body, flails her fists, begins to scream in misery, just as the jelly begins to boil. There is nothing for it but to take Bess up, jounce her on a hip *(there, there)* and with her one free hand frantically skim and ladle. *There, there.* The batch is poured and capped and sealed, all one-handed, jiggling-hipped. There, there, it is done.

Anna's knees begin to tremble. No, she dare not sit. *You know if you set down you'll never make yourself get up again.* One of the jelly glasses has burst; the amber drips onto the floor, has to be mopped; and Bess still to be hushed. *Hush you, hush, you'll wake every sleeping one, there, there,* transferring her to the other hip and one-handed sponging her again and her own sweating face as well. *There there, poor baby.* The tenderness mixes with a compulsion of exhaustion to have done, to put Bess outside in the yard where she can scream and scream outside of hearing and Anna can be free to splash herself with running water, forget the canning and the kids and sink into a chair, lay her forehead on the table and do nothing. *There there Bessie, there there, we'll go out a spell, see what's outside,* fixing a sun shade for the baby out of a soaked dish towel.

The stink, the stink. What glares so? The air is feverish; it lies in a stagnant swill of heat haze over the river and tracks below. Anna gags, turns to go back in from the stench and swelter, but Bess has quieted, is reaching her arms to the air. Giant cracks have opened in the earth. At her feet she sees her garden is dying; each plant in its own manner, each plant known and dear to her, blackening or curling or shriveling or blotching. "I aint had time, I'm sorry," she whispered. "The water's savin for sundown watering time. And maybe nothing coulda helped. *There there Bessie.* I cant stand here and keep being shade for you neither," thinking with bowed head of the dying crops—corn and wheat and tomatoes and beans—and farmers' families drooping in the miles and miles of baking prairie. "Burning all over, Bessie," she said, "Kansas and Dakota and Ioway too," and went to fetch the saved water. The first pail ran off as if off clay, the earth refusing to absorb. The second pail she sloshed slowly, still one-handed *(there there, Bessie),* breaking the flow over her grateful feet, red and swollen from the all-day standing. The water sinking into the dried earth seemed to sink into something parched and drought-eaten in her as well. "We have to go in, baby," she said, "we'll scorch," but stood there in the mud-feet coolness and the blister air, making the slenderest shade over the tomato plants. Stinging dust, spitting up suddenly from a quick hot wind, took her by surprise. She covered Bess's face, saw that great columns of dust-wraiths were swirling across the river and down the street. *There, there;* Bess's body relaxed into sleep. The furnace wind was gone as suddenly as it came, though dust still moved through the again stagnant air. Washing her feet in the kitchen, she saw in astonishment a thick dust frosting on the caked mud; dust pitted in every visible pore of her legs and arms. All had settled outside; inside her sleepers slept. She started back on the peaches.

Five o'clock. Still 107°.

Mazie half wakes from her sweated sleep; her mother is sponging her, calling her name urgently over and over. "You been sleeping so long I got worried; everytime I looked in on you, you seemed sleeping. Are you all right? I cant tell is it fever or this heat? Tell me, where is it hurts? . . ."

Still the need to slither along the floor; douse, rid herself of her vast billowing head.

Somehow on the couch in the kitchen beside Ben, head to his feet, feet to his head. The sun is slanting its long last rays through the window. An iridescence floats on her hand, rainbows the wall, shifts in scales of hue here and there in the room. What is it, what is it? The hanging prism? One of the rays, touching it, has cracked open; burst; unfolded the radiance. The other rays still slant unbroken—straight shafts of light, clear threads of glass. Are the rainbows, the floating pools, the radiance folded into each one of them too? Where kept? How hidden? The wonder dazes her head and she turns her hand to hold the stammering light, unlock its magic, but she grasps shadows, and the iridescence glides onto Ben's unconscious face.

Not knowing an every-hued radiance floats on her hair, her mother stands at the sink; her knife seems flying. Fruit flies rise and settle and rise.

Lovingly: "Momma."

"It's the last batch," she answers. "Are you alright?" Smiling with the happiness of the worst not having happened. "Benjy's better too. Wait, soon I can sponge you . . . Can you drink something or try a little sugar bread?"

Jim does not stagger nor waddle coming in; it is more a hitching, straight for the sink—turns the water on full force, gulping great draughts, submerging his face, dousing himself. Red, boiled; under the faucet blowing his walrusy spray. Grabbing the watering bucket and splashing it over himself, filling and refilling it, pouring it over his body.

Running for a towel to wipe him, a pitcher she can fill and a glass to drink from, some relief she can give him. ("Jimmie run to Kryckszis quick and ask ice for poppa.") Anna thinks: hating herself for thinking: the water, the water; the money, the parched waiting garden, the mess to be cleaned; will it be one more, Jim bad-sick too? and begs: "What happened, Jim? What's the matter?"

But Jim lies as if he were drunk, out by the stoop in the evening shadow, sousing himself with sponge and the pail water, and will not speak.

Seven o'clock. Heat lightning. 106°.

Still Jim lies on his water-soaked pallet below the stoop, but he sleeps now, snoring, twitching his hands.

Ben shifts around to lie in Mazie's arms—not too close, for it is so hot. "'Splain to me about bad dreams," he whispers into her ear, "tell me about boogie mans and scaredies and ghosts and hell."

Flies bumble and fry in the lamp; peach and amber

jars of jelly and fruit cover every surface. Anna sits at last, holding Bess at the kitchen table, singing with heat-cracked lips "I Saw a Ship a-Sailing," waiting for Will to come home so that the lights can go out and the trying-to-sleep time can begin again. *I Saw a Ship . . .* It is all heat delirium and near suffocation now.

Bang!

Bess who has been fingering a fruit-jar lid—absently, heedlessly dropped it—aimlessly groping across the table, reclaims it again. Lightning in her brain. She releases, grabs, releases, grabs. I can do. Bang! I did that. I can do. I! A look of neanderthal concentration is on her face. That noise! In triumphant, astounded joy she clashes the lid down. Bang, slam, whack. Release, grab, slam, bang, bang. Centuries of human drive work in her; human ecstasy of achievement; satisfaction deep and fundamental as sex: *I can do, I use my powers; I! I!* Wilder, madder, happier the bangs. The fetid fevered air rings with Anna's, Mazie's, Ben's laughter; Bess's toothless, triumphant crow. Heat misery, rash misery transcended.

And Will comes in to the laughter with coils and boxes and a long, long wire. One by one, on the Metzes borrowed crystal set, they hear for the first time the radio sound. From where, from where, thinks Mazie, floating on her pain; like the spectrum in the ray, the magic concealed; *and hears in her ear the veering transparent meshes of sound, far sound, human and stellar, pulsing, pulsing. . . .*

Dust blows up and, stinging, flings itself against the house. Anna imagines the great dust wraiths swirling again, goes to wake Jim and urge him in. Trees move in the furnace wind, in the lightning quiver. She yearns to be out into it.

"Jim, wake up. Come in. This dust . . . Bess . . . Mazie . . . The radio . . . Willie borried a crystal set."

He is too dazed to listen.

"Come in, get freshened up. Here, I'll help you. The air's changin, Jim. I see for it to end tomorrow, at least get tolerable. Come in."

Reader, it was not to have ended here, but it is nearly forty years since this book had to be set aside, never to come to completion.

These pages you have read are all that is deemed publishable of it. Only fragments, rough drafts, outlines, scraps remain—to tell what might have been, and never will be now.

Yonnondio! Yonnondio! —unlimn'd they disappear.

A Note About This Book

This book, conceived primarily as a novel of the 1930's, was begun in 1932 in Faribault, Minnesota, when the author was nineteen, and worked on intermittently into 1936 or perhaps 1937 in Omaha, Stockton, Venice (Calif.), Los Angeles and San Francisco. Unfinished, it yet bespeaks the consciousness and roots of that decade, if not its events.

Thought long since lost or destroyed, some of its pages were found intermixed with other old papers last winter, during the process of searching for another manuscript. A later, more thorough, search turned up additional makings: odd tattered pages, lines in yellowed notebooks, scraps. Other parts, evidently once in existence, seem irrevocably lost.

The first four chapters, in final or near-final form when fitted together, presented only minor problems. The succeeding pages were increasingly difficult to reclaim. There were usually two to fourteen versions to work from: 38 to 41 year old penciled-over scrawls and fragments to decipher and piece together. Judgment had to be exercised as to which version, revision or draft to choose or combine; decision made whether to include or omit certain first drafts and notes; and guessing as to where several scenes belonged. In this sense—the choices and omissions, the combinings and reconstruction—the book ceased to be solely the work of that long ago young writer and, in arduous partnership, became this older one's as well. But it is all the old manuscripts—no rewriting, no new writing.

I wish to thank the MacDowell Colony for the solitude and protection which enabled me to work on this during five months of 1972 and into 1973.

TILLIE OLSEN

San Francisco, February 1973

BIOGRAPHIES OF TWO BRILLIANT
TWENTIETH CENTURY WRITERS

☐ **COLETTE**
The Difficulty of Loving
Margaret Crosland 3350-00

A penetrating biography of the writer many critics and readers feel to be France's greatest woman novelist. This work unclouds the accepted legends surrounding Colette and explores the writer and the woman. "The best biography yet of this willful, difficult, talented woman."—*The New York Times*. "It is nothing less than an essay on talent, that central mystery which enables the artist to subdue events, people and words . . . This is a work which respects the essential integrity of Colette."—*Los Angeles Times* $1.25

☐ **MALCOLM LOWRY**
Douglas Day 5250-06

A remarkable portrait of the prodigal, clumsy, and shy genius who wrote one of this century's great novels. This biography contains extensive criticism of Lowry's work as well as the account of his chaotic and tragic life and his more than thirty years as an alcoholic. "The finest biography I have read this year—perceptive, comprehensive, closely analytical and genuinely enlightening."—*John Barkham*. Douglas Day's account of Malcolm Lowry's novel UNDER THE VOLCANO "is a model of its kind, perhaps the most complete and useful critique of the structure, style, subject matter and intentions of that work." —*The Washington Post Book World* $2.25

Winner of the *1974 National Book Award* for Biography

Laurel  *Editions*